Wild Gestures

Wild Gestures

STORIES

by

LUCY DURNEEN

To Alpha Sister
Maria,
So happy the
Trannis [illegible]
continue to
carry the words
across oceans.

MidnightSun

First published 2017 by MidnightSun Publishing Pty Ltd
PO Box 3647, Rundle Mall, SA 5000, Australia.
www.midnightsunpublishing.com

Cataloguing-in-Publication entry is available from the
National Library of Australia.
http://catalogue.nla.gov.au

Cover design by Kim Lock
Internal design by Zena Shapter

Printed and bound in Australia by Griffin Press. The papers used by MidnightSun in the manufacture of this book are natural, recyclable products made from wood grown in sustainable plantation forests.

For Sam, Charlie, Oliver and Eliza,

for Freeborn,

and

the great (and wild) G.P.

Contents

Icarus' daughter

I was the child who took to the sky
with wax paper wings to carry her by,
and lift her as she learned to fly.

I was the girl who harnessed the air,
and spoke the love-language of despair,
to find there was no-one to hold her there.

I am the woman who fell to the sea
Its sounds replace the rhythms of me,
which leaves me drowning, constantly.

Time is a river without banks

Not even the so-called elements are constant.

Listen, and I will tell you of their changes.

Ovid; *Metamorphoses.*

The beauty of the house was not in any doubt. It was small compared to the last place, but it had views. Some renovation was needed, which the agent said meant it had potential to add value: interested parties should try to see beyond the flock and the linoleum, and certainly ought not to be afraid of damp. Damp was something you just had to live with in this part of the country. If you couldn't live with damp, the agent wanted to say, there would be other, more fundamental things you would not be able to live with around here.

The couple that came to view the house had been married a long time but they had only just now had a baby. It had been a struggle, that was what the mother told people, and she meant more than just the fight to conceive. The father told people that now they were looking to settle, it was time to put down roots. Every time he said it the mother felt she was living in a way that was nothing like the conscious way in which human beings are alive, as if she had no choice but to simply grow and flower, and so putting down roots, gripping hold of the ground, was simply an effort not to die.

The agent was right about the house needing work but the father felt it was an appropriate amount according to his equation, which was based on ten per cent returns, and good enough in this market. The walls were silver and damp, and the mother looked beyond them and imagined how the baby would sit on the kitchen floor banging pots and pans together. In some rooms the walls were mottled as fish skin. But they kept on walking round the house and the mother kept saying how good it was that they could add value. The father tickled the baby under the chin and the mother went back and ran her hands over the wallpaper, asking herself if she could live with it for as long as it took and deciding that she could, she probably could.

The couple were impressed by the garden and the French windows in the sitting room, which let in a glut of light and made the mother feel heavy just to stand there, as if the weight of the light had compressed her in some way. There were only two bedrooms, but this was okay because it had taken so long for the baby that the mother in particular did not want to go through all that again. But when she walked into what would be the baby's bedroom, the mother saw something that she didn't like quite so much.

'Did this used to be an entrance?' she asked the agent. 'It

looks like it might have been an old entrance to the house.'

'It's got steps down to the garden,' the agent said, throwing open the door onto a wooden balcony. The balcony spread the length of the first floor and there were woods in the distance, a dark mineral green, a dimness of mist, then sky. The sky was strapped to the land by a flash of water. Then the mother could see that it was not water but in fact more sky, deep and flooding above the tops of the trees.

'It could be a real feature,' the agent said. 'If you did it up, this balcony would definitely add value.'

'What are we talking?' the father said. 'Five, ten thousand?'

'Oh no,' said the mother. 'No, we couldn't have that. I just can't help but think, "what if someone climbed up those steps and got in during the night?" Into the baby's room. I don't think I could sleep worrying someone might get in.'

The father said, 'Are you serious?'

'It's a safe neighbourhood,' the agent said. 'You just don't hear of things like that happening here.'

'Maybe not round here,' said the mother, and her husband knew she was thinking of the two girls in the town where she grew up. But still he said, 'See, it's not a problem.'

'I don't know,' the mother said and you could tell by the way she went over to the door and touched the handle that she really didn't. 'I just can't help but think of it. It's all I would think of.' She slipped her little finger inside the key hole, felt how it could turn or hold fast if there was someone on the other side. She said, 'What if the baby opens the door herself when she gets bigger? Can you imagine if she fell?'

'It's okay,' the father said. 'We can nail it shut or something. We could, right?' he said, looking at the agent. The agent, who was young and indifferent, said probably they could. They would lose the feature, but yes they could do that. She said this in such a way that made it sound obscene and the mother felt a quiet rage against all the people of the world who had no fear except for the loss of features and value. The mother didn't look at the agent. She inspected the frame of the door, how it would give way, understood the urgent desire its opening would invite in. She knew she probably ought to, but the mother would not look at the estate agent.

'Wouldn't you prefer to put a table and chairs out here?' the agent said. 'It would be an incredible feature.'

They all stood for a moment, looking at the woods far off at the edge of the moorland that touched the back garden, which you would be able to see if the door was open and there were a table and chairs on the balcony. The mother felt a pulling sensation, as if she needed to swim or as if the next step would take her ten feet in the air. Then the baby gurgled and it was as if the memory of the earth had never left her. She was thinking of other things now. 'Since when could you tell a shovel from a tyre iron?' the mother asked, because she knew her husband, and she hadn't married him for his practical skills.

'I'll get someone in,' he said. 'I want this house. I think it's going to make a damn fine investment.'

'But what about a damn fine home?'

'Sure. That too.'

⁂

They had two vans deliver the furniture from their rented house and still the father had to go back for odds and ends, boxes of things that were his wife's alone, a microscopic version of her childhood that she kept sealed up and protected. He asked himself more than once if all women did this. Of the women he had loved, she was the only one with such nostalgia. He put the boxes straight up into the attic and he didn't look in them. He didn't think she ever looked in the boxes. But it was important they knew everything was there, that the things inside were like an anchor, grounding her.

The father got a man in to fix the door straight away. As time went on his wife would begin to think of other, necessary things for the future, such as home-schooling and a reliable internet connection, but for now it was just the door and the father wanted to get on with it, to show her he meant what he said. He watched how the handyman first battened across the architraves with lengths of 2x4 and then boarded the doorway with sheets of Gyprock. It was as if the door to the balcony had never been there. The father had no idea if it was the correct way to do it but the man had all the right tools and he worked fast, and that had to count for something. 'Good job, Roberto,' he said, hardly knowing what he was thanking the handyman for. You couldn't see the door and you couldn't open the door, which was what he had paid him to do when it came to it. But if you looked up at the house from the outside you could see the sealed shadow of where the door had been, and ghoulishly it reminded the handyman, who was from Umbria, of the doors of the dead that were found in old Italian houses.

'You know I love you,' the mother said to her husband when she came up to the room to put the baby to bed. 'You do, don't you?'

'You can't see the door any more,' the father said, touching the wall with a professional sweep as if he had done the work himself.

'What about window locks?' the mother said. 'Do you think we should have some of those too?' She looked out across the moor to the woods where the trees had disappeared, evening out the landscape as though the dark had simply pressed down into the shape of the world and removed them. Always she felt the need to keep the woods out. It seemed that in the dark there was no way of telling anything that might happen in the world and if everything that was solid and ancient outside could dissolve, then so might she. The mother thought it couldn't be a coincidence so many deaths and births occur at night. She put the baby in the cot and pulled the blankets snug. The baby moved in a slow arc towards the top of the cot and the mother put out her hand, felt the curve of her daughter's head like an egg cupped into her palm.

'He's done a grand job,' she said to her husband. 'There's not a chance anyone's getting in or out now.'

But the father said nothing. He pushed her against the wall where there was no longer a door; gently, so he could kiss her. But he did not then kiss in a gentle way. It was nice to kiss like that, for a change. The mother didn't say it, but surprise was the only way to describe it, yes. She could still see out of the window, towards the stillness of the woods where there were no lights and no people. Everything outside the window was the colour of indigo and bone. She felt the stillness like a fluid substance. Like water it seeped through the snag of roots, from branch to branch; it found a gap into the open air, pushed through a suffocation of pine limbs. The stillness rushed across the moor and the garden, licking the footings of the house and the balcony, as if they might be afloat. Little, buoyant airs nudged around the mother's arms and beneath her feet. 'Did you hear that noise?' she said. 'The baby.' Her husband's voice came as if it were inside her, swimming like a cell in her blood, pushing through muscle and bone. She felt it deep in the savage hollow of her belly. Every beat of her heart was a word. 'There's no noise,' he was saying. 'No noise.'

When the morning came the mother realised they must have fallen asleep right there on the floor. The sunrise felt like the surprise of the Earth at finding itself still here in the solar system. The red of the sun was ancient and the shock was stratospheric, pushing out through the whole sky.

'The windows,' the mother said. 'I don't know.'

'I can ask Roberto to board them out,' the father said into her neck. 'If you want me to, I can do that.'

They had been in the house a while and the baby was about ten, although sometimes the mother felt she wasn't quite sure that so many years had passed. The market had changed somewhat and the potential to add value to the house was not what it had been, but nothing remains the same, and the mother was glad somehow that the world had woken up to that. Yet in other ways everything remained as it had been. They continued to do all the same things they had done in their rented house but it turned out that putting down roots meant those things now seemed real, as if they had just been rehearsing before. Sometimes the mother wanted to shout: 'this lasagne is fabulous!' Or, 'look how clean the floor is!' as if those were lines she had only been practising in that earlier time, holding them in until the right time came. There were whole days when the mother wondered exactly what it was they had been doing before, as if it had all been about waiting, like ancient fish just biding their time until fins became legs and they could walk or run.

To make up for the fact there were no longer any views from the baby's bedroom the mother, who had been to art college, pinned up bunting cut from triangles of rainbow cotton and covered the walls with prints of famous paintings; mainly Chagall, some Kahlo; there had been a Picasso that gave the daughter nightmares. Every morning the mother would come into her daughter's room and say, 'I love you, what do you need? More toast? Something to read?'

'I'm okay,' her daughter said more often than not, because it was just a routine; there was no real requirement for her to want more toast or have a desire to read anything. The daughter was dark-haired, which was the way of all the women on the father's side of the family, and her head looked too heavy for her shoulders, which was also like her father from some angles. Of her mother's heritage there was really very little visible sign, which the mother found hard at times, as if she had failed to assert her own biology, which should have been such a simple thing.

'Always my baby girl,' the mother said, tidying shelves, straightening a book. It felt like a question, sometimes. Sometimes her daughter answered, yes; sometimes she didn't.

The mother liked to look at the paintings with her

daughter. It didn't matter that they were just copies and you could only guess at the passion of the brushstrokes or how the artist had pushed the paint around the canvas. It became a way to pass time that felt more truthful than hands moving around a clock face. The father especially was proud that his daughter's first word had been *impasto*.

'This one is my favourite,' the mother said. 'It's called *The Birthday*. See how much the man and woman adore each other? Even the room is too small for them. It's like the city outside is calling to them. It's like the sky is asking them to come and explore.' She wanted to say something more. This one is about love, she wanted to say. I love you this way, baby girl. In another picture a fish swam amongst the stars. In another, a cat transformed into a woman, a cockerel carried a bride towards the Garden of Eden. It was hard to know how to explain that. She was almost surprised to learn that her daughter had her own words for the paintings. She watched her daughter walk from one picture to another and say things like, 'It's sad, though, that even on their birthday the man and woman don't belong in the room.' The mother thought about this. 'But see how they're looking at each other,' she said. 'They belong together. That's what counts.'

'Can I play outside?' the daughter asked, bored.

'We talked about this,' the mother said, remembering how they needed to fix the gate after storms had blown in the posts. 'We already said no.'

Suddenly the mother could see her daughter walking down their driveway onto the lane joining the main road into town. She heard cars. She could feel the darkness of the space under the cars, the darkness of bruises, and blood, so much blood. She felt euphoric in her refusal. 'No', she said again. Then she said, 'Would you like to use the computer? We could look up something.'

'Like what?'

'Like anything in the world.'

Two clicks and they were there. Anywhere. Click, click. The mother clicked through radiant pages of blue buildings and white mountains, and it seemed that life was wild and a dream and a blaze; she was wild, she herself was a dream. She was dizzy under the crash of distant waves and for a moment she was not a mother but an ordinary girl, not even a girl, a child, something yet to be, a spray of atoms. Less than that. She was just a single atom. Less than *that*. Her existence was merely potential. The feeling of being such a trivial part of the universe was like being caught in the eye of a strong wind. Then a sudden nausea hit. The nausea made it difficult to stand or even sit straight, as if she was filling up with air, and the mother put her arms around her daughter and felt how light she was, how she felt like crumpled paper, or a balloon. The lightness of her daughter did not make it any easier. She wanted to call out for her husband. Her husband, she guessed, would be outside. In one of the gardens along the lane a dog barked. The mother did not move. She thought fiercely of the boxes in the attic. She went through the contents one by one, a mental audit of books, photographs, train tickets, until the nausea began to subside. She felt her daughter put out her hand and reach for the keys of the computer, how she carried on clicking and searching, but just out of view. As if the mother did not know her, or as if her daughter did not want to be known.

❧

It was winter and the nights began to come in fast, rushing out of the forest like fire. The mother went to bed earlier than usual, suspended under the duvet in a state that was more intense even than wakefulness, until her husband crept in beside her. From under her cover it was like watching some very small, very urgent animal move across the forest floor; you could only tell where it had been and not where it was. It never occurred to her husband that she was not asleep and so he couldn't disturb her.

'I heard something,' the mother said one night, sitting up straight. 'Would you go and see?'

'Go back to sleep,' the father said. 'Go on.'

'It was like something thumping,' the mother said. 'You must have heard it.' But the father hadn't. The mother tried to describe the sound but in the dark she found her words were inadequate; there was no correlation between the sounds that could be offered as words and the sound that she had heard. Again, no. Her husband had no inkling of there having been any kind of noise. 'I'll make you a warm drink,' he said, but his eyes were closed and the mother did not want a drink anyway. The noise was still there, distantly, like you would remember a noise years after an event when it was no longer something you could hear but more a thing you could summon, like poetry. She supposed this was how a newly deaf person might still be able to recall the sound of a lover's voice. In this way she followed the sound to her daughter's bedroom. She opened the door, pressed her toes into the carpet, saw the walls and the furniture fill the vacuum of the places they had always been.

In the darkness the mother ran her hands along the wall where ten years before there had been a door, and windows. There was a ridge where the frame might once have interrupted the smoothness of the brickwork. For the first time the mother could sense its oddness. It was a broken bone under new skin. If it was possible to feel sadness for something as ordinary as a wall, she was feeling it, in her temples and across her forehead, like a fever. Some people would call it a migraine but the mother knew it was more than that. It was the sadness of the whole world. It was the sadness of every room where people didn't belong. She sat on the bed, which was empty, but the mother had known this before she looked; she had already rehearsed this moment, the burst behind her rib cage was familiar, old, it was not even a feeling but an instinct, or a damaged kind of bravery. She stood up again to look at the paintings, which did not look like the same pictures that could be seen in the day. She stared at the cold colours. This panic, she thought, this love. This child.

And then abruptly the mother saw her, soaring high above a gabled roof. At first it seemed that the daughter was going to fly directly into, or maybe out of, the frame, but at the last minute she turned and dove as if into water, her legs bent a little at the knee, her body unembarrassed by its fall. The daughter's legs seemed to be telling her to let go. Each kick into the air took her further away. She rounded a church spire. Trees rose and receded. There were yellow houses, then a whole town. More and more details flooded into the foreground but the daughter kept flying over the town, as if she didn't want to land. The mother waved in fear. But for a minute she also marvelled at what her daughter could do. Now her daughter torpedoed towards the trees. Now she coasted out over the river. The river below her daughter's feet was old, it had seen wars, but now it dozed, now it slept.

The mother went up close to the picture and touched the surface. Her fingers shook as they made contact. They covered first the door of a barn, then a small duck in the foreground. She opened her hands and spread her fingers wide. Nothing seemed to have changed, but there was her daughter. She stepped back and the wider perspective only made it clearer.

Later the mother would recall a look on the daughter's face that she couldn't place, or perhaps hadn't quite seen because of the angle of her flight. She would try and explain it to people who would listen, but the mother was now reduced to a language of absence, which made no sense to the people who could still celebrate presence in conventional ways. It was not like a hole had opened up in the world, the mother would say. It was not like that world was any different; everyone still had somewhere to get to, she still had floors to clean, and the gas bill, although she stopped making lasagne. It was a little like birth, the mother said, which she had been afraid of, but survived. That was the closest the mother would come. She would try to tell her husband, when he was taking down the Gyprock and the 2x4 battens: she would try to tell him how it seemed that in the painting the whole of the sky was flowing through their daughter and everything she knew to be solid was being exchanged, as if the sky was a feeling, as if the sky was life and only their daughter could see exactly what that meant.

Noli me tangere

There was an accident at the public beach and the boy from the hotel, breathless with the effort to convey urgency, suggested they went down to the promenade to look. If they didn't go now, he seemed to be explaining, there would be no spectacle, the ambulances would come, a cordon erected. Alicia couldn't really tell the details, because of the accent, but that was why there were international signs. When she flipped him the bird he looked almost pleased. The rumour was that a tourist had come off a pedalo; it was *essenziale* they didn't leave it more than a few minutes if they were going to see anything.

'You want excite?' the boy from the hotel asked. He reached to take Alicia's hand, briefly, dangerously, lacing their fingers together in a way that left dark streaks against the naked whiteness of her thumbs. To clinch the deal the boy threw in the fact they could get *gelato* afterwards. They wouldn't have to buy it, he explained, because his sister was going to marry Marco who worked at one of the *gelateria* in the piazza Matteotti. The boy's English was pretty bad, or almost good depending on whether you could tune in. The story he told her involved Marco and the sister's best friend but in a way that made Marco seem like a good guy, like a hero. 'I feel bad for Anna,' he said, suddenly shy. 'But ice cream forever—is good!'

Alicia didn't really know him, the boy. Just twice they had spoken, once when he carried their bags from the hotel lobby to their room and again when the air conditioning broke. She liked the way his face changed at her mother's coldness, his visible surprise that she could be so angry about such a small thing. She noticed how he avoided looking over her mother's shoulder, away towards the balcony from where she, Alicia, was watching and she liked that too, how studiously he ignored the pale shine of her stomach, her legs, the new and unfamiliar parts of her that were on show this summer, how the lack of interest seemed to be a different kind of interest. It was more exciting. What she did not expect: it was just *more*, like the way dark matter was there even if it couldn't be proved. 'I'm here!' she wanted to shout. But the not looking was like answering. Out on the balcony it was like not being there. It was like the whole room was very far away, only a few things connecting her to it, like a skin, or another person's memory; the hum of the bathroom fan, a guava, green and unripe in the fruit bowl. Some kind of bite irritating the white quadrants behind her knees. There wasn't a word she knew for that part of you, a part you could touch but had to make an effort to see, and that was annoying. She was really worried about European hornets but they hadn't seen any, so.

Ten minutes later she had seen the boy walking fast across

the terrace, his body upright and angry, like an animal. He kicked a stone that landed in the swimming pool. Then he looked up, at their balcony, shaded his eyes against the sun. They stood quietly, as if maybe neither one of them were there. The evening breeze came and lifted her skirt, only a little at first, and then wilder, so she had to smooth it down. But the boy said nothing. He stared up at the balcony a little longer. She stared down at him, but as if she was looking at the trees, or the air mattress that someone had left, floating like a dark island, like a nothingness, between the shadows. An archipelago of pine needles drifted past. She dreamed about the boy that night and in her dream she was the water of the pool, felt the hard descent of the stone as it split her open.

When he asked her to go down to the promenade she thought; so this is what it feels like. Love. It felt less incredible than she had imagined. To be honest, it felt more like the start of Mono, or her period. He mocked going down on his knees and then she remembered a third time when they had met but not spoken, when he had been tying his shoelaces in the corridor, when he hadn't noticed her. She pretended to think about it. 'OK. Give me *excite*,' she said, presenting her hand like they were about to dance, hoping it sounded like an order, which was the way her mother spoke and how she got people to listen. 'But forget the ice cream. Today's a fast day. A *fast* day. Never mind.'

❧

He moved in a way she hadn't seen other boys move, as

though he belonged to a different element, which right away was a thought that embarrassed her. Did she think he was some kind of ghost? His hand at the small of her back, urging her through the crowded street, felt real enough, but only in the way you just have to trust that anything's real. There was that verb she used in her mid-term English paper, the one that got her a commendation for lexical inventiveness—hieing. He hied through the streets, winged. A vapour, a mercury flash. Was he even a boy? Half a man. Crowds parted for him, melted for him. 'Wait!' she shouted, falling behind. Suddenly there was the stink of feathers, a rapid change in the movement of the air. Again the air shuddered with the beating of wings. In an open marquee filled with trestle tables bright parakeets quarrelled in wire cages. Tourists, molten skinned, walked a sweating corridor of love birds, frantic in their flightless dash east to west. 'Luis!' Alicia called after him. 'Luis, wait, I lost you.'

'*Luca*,' the boy shouted back, curving in and out of the crowd to where she stood frowning in at the lovebirds. 'My name is Luca.'

'You live on the second floor?'

'What?'

'Nothing. It's just a song.'

It was just a song that he didn't know, which made it another way in which the facts could masquerade as mystery. They had nothing in common. But they could shrug it off. Later she might write home about it on one of the hotel postcards. It wasn't like it could become their song, not a song like that, but it would be something cool.

'*Sagra dei Osei*,' was the boy's explanation. 'The Festival of

Birds.' He was trying to pick up speed but they couldn't get past a woman who took up half the street with an entourage of canvas bags and some kind of terrier snapping on a halti. The heat didn't do the woman any favours, freckling her upper lip with perspiration and cola. 'Get our picture, Grace,' she was saying to her companion and she meant herself and the dog. 'Make sure those pretty fish are in behind. Not the goddamn kids.' It was okay, because Grace would crop out the goddamn kids once they were home. But it was a bad shot anyway, Alicia could see that. It would be a shot of a fish tank on a trestle table while a fat woman sweated over a tiny dog, the whole thing inexplicable once viewed in an album. With the defiant confidence of the talentless, Grace shot through ten different poses; there was nowhere to go until it was over. Being cropped out would be a relief, Alicia thought, it would be like giving her permission to ignore how incredible it was that the boy didn't seem to feel the sadness of the birds in the cages. He petted a gasping rabbit fenced in to a square foot of gravel and she could have thrown up.

'You want to touch this bird?' the boy asked her, stopping at one of the tables. He spoke in a low voice to the vendor and Alicia could see where the woman's brassiere bit into her skin and also where once something had cut like a soft white bracelet across the flesh of her upper arm. 'Jesus, no!' she said, but the bird was on her anyway, attached to the vendor's wrist by a narrow chain, equally reluctant to be held. It flapped once, and then set up a little march on the back of her hand.

The lightness of the bird was surprising, the tiny scrape of its feet as it shifted up and down. There was a girl at school who'd gotten pregnant last year and whose body, when she returned to class, made the same apology, permanently curved into an embarrassed caesura as if she wanted only half of her to be visible at any one time. Alicia wouldn't meet the bird's gaze. But it didn't seem like the bird cared. Again the feeling came; love was also a complicated kind of revulsion. 'Tell her to get it off me!' she said and the boy's laugh was off-beam, like it had come from the back of a theatre at what is meant to be a moment of silent, poetic intensity. 'We go, yes?' he said, tilting his wrist so his watch, a cheap imitation of something that was supposed to indicate status, caught the sun.

'But don't you think it's weird,' she said after they had walked away, the boy hurrying her along with his hand at her back. 'The way they're running. The birds. Didn't you see how they're all running in the direction of the lake?'

He didn't think it was weird. But he did think they should walk faster.

By the time they reached the Boat Hire there were already reporters there and *poliziotti* thinning out the crowd, but for the quick there were still ways in and the boy navigated with the proficiency of a person well-practised at making things disappear fast. From the pale green lawns of the promenade holidaymakers watched the water move about the figures of two police divers. What nobody was talking about was how cold the water actually was even with the heatwave. But it meant the piazza cafes were busier than normal and under the striped awnings ink-haired waitresses, proving how tragedy brings out the most expensive of human impulses, served whole bottles of Barolo and didn't comment on the way their customers were updating their social media even as the divers made another ascent to the lake's surface alone. Most of those gathered had a version of what they were doing when the incident happened. But almost nobody could explain the boat's sudden lurch, or the way, for just a moment, the tourist had been observed standing quite still, frozen in an elongated present tense where they were neither falling nor sitting, but breathing and smiling, until the water hit.

The lake swelled and sank, rolled like a glass ball. Like a fisheye it blinked, like a mouth it swallowed. The rise of blue, the falling blue, was regular as breathing. It was a shame how you couldn't call things cerulean any more if you wanted to be the kind of person who didn't use clichés. To Alicia the water looked so light, so impossibly, intangibly light, but inside it was the solid fact of the tourist, hidden somewhere in darkness, and behind Mount Baldo threw long shadows into the sky, pink and yellow towns clinging to its foothills the way an uncertain suicide, pockets lined with stones, might wait with one foot suspended above the water, unsure of the desire to drown. A forest of weed swayed at the shoreline. The breeze pulled the weed one way, then another, and back, and then Alicia was doing it too, this instinctive dance where she was entirely unaware of her own lunging movement, which was how her aunt, a teacher, had once described swaying in front of her students after her maternity leave, rocking an imaginary infant to prolong every second of quiet.

'Too bad we see nothing,' the boy said, breaking the spell. 'I said we have to be quick.'

'Shit. You think he drowned?'

He shrugged. 'Not he. A woman.'

It was worse that way, somehow. As if even the Earth had not bothered to do the gallant thing. They stood in silence for a minute, watching a tall man shouting on the jetty steps and she wondered if later this would be the moment people spoke of as having changed everything, and how sad it was that it didn't feel any different at all from the moment before or after. Alicia threw a stone into the jellied skin of the water, which was only a small thing but at least it was a thing. The falling feeling got her again, the one like in her dream, only this time she was going faster, being pulled almost, into the dark and the water sealed above her, tight, like someone had mended a drum. But it was just the drift of the branches overhead after all. They were in the light. They were in shadow. The light came back again, like an obscene, forgotten secret.

The boy seemed to be listening to something. He turned to her, put his hands square on her shoulders and said, 'You want to go?'

'Go where?'

'Is over. *Polizia di Stato* are coming. From the city. You want ice cream now?'

'Jesus!' she said, the nausea building. 'I already told you no ice cream. And what do you mean it's over?'

She didn't want ice cream, but the need for something to take away the weighted feeling in her stomach made Alicia feel a little crazy. 'You smoke?' the boy asked but she shook her head. Where the promenade gave way to the main piazza was a café where two half-drunk bottles of Peroni sat on an otherwise empty table. 'Take them', Alicia told the boy, *take them*, and mimed drinking from the bottle. But he wouldn't, so she grabbed them herself and in a street two minutes march away slumped down against a warm stucco wall and waited for him to catch up. From ten yards she tossed him one of the bottles, some kind of confirmation that she was entirely at ease with the thing that she knew for sure was going to happen next, because this was what death, or the thought of death, made you do. The boy caught the flash of amber by the neck. She could tell he wanted to kiss her and she kept the bottle with the most left to drink, in case she lost her nerve.

It was hard to know what things to talk about. The boy aped a toast, drained his bottle, then looked up brightly. 'You like football?'

'Like, soccer? No.'

'Movies?'

'Yeah.'

'Not ice cream.'

'That's just a thing. It's a fast day.'

'But you like how you look, yes?'

'I guess.'

Alicia was surprised he asked this. Liking how you looked seemed obvious, the way, once found, you can only ever see the picture in a Magic Eye and not the coloured dots around it. One day she had looked in the mirror and there was a girl, a pretty girl, not so much hidden as just previously unseen, camouflaged in plain sight, and she wanted to protect her. It was that simple. It was women, not men, who found the idea of beauty interesting, she realised this, but even so.

'Here we say this,' the boy said. '*La bellezza va e viene—la bontà si mantiene.* It means, beauty doesn't last, kindness is forever.'

'You saying I'm vain?'

The boy assured her, he definitely was not saying she was vain. What he seemed not to understand was that no-one gave a fuck about an ugly girl. But he didn't feel like the sort of person you could say that to and she still wanted him to like her, or maybe needed him to, which was not quite the same thing but under the circumstances was what her father would have called *good enough for government work*.

'What will happen now?' she asked the boy, tilting the beer bottle in the direction of the lake. 'Are they like, removing her body?'

'I don't know.'

'But did they actually find her?'

'I don't know!'

'Is there maybe a chance that she'll be okay?'

'Maybe a chance, yes.'

'What do you think it feels like to drown?'

'Alice,' the boy said, abruptly. 'My English is not so good for this.'

She bent over to fix something on her shoe. Lately her body had started doing this new thing when she wanted to cry, becoming unbearably heavy so that it was not embarrassment but weight that eventually broke her, which felt exactly the same as when she tried a particularly complex piece on the piano and her fingers just couldn't move fast enough. It was actually a very basic problem; just an instantaneous feeling of being terribly small in a vast world, which sometimes could be more beautiful than you knew what to do with. Sometimes even a rapidly ascending series of arpeggios could be too much. She didn't know even one word of Italian capable of explaining it.

'You promised me *excite*,' Alicia said to the boy instead, throwing back the end of the Peroni. 'So show me something exciting.'

❧

There were the Scaligeri ruins, not as extensive or complete as elsewhere in the region, but about the right amount for how much he knew and how interested she was in medieval history. The rumour of ghosts would have been a better story had it been dark. They walked streets bright with white tremors of bougainvillea. At the point the beach gave way to damp groves of cypress, three girls were cutting a path the colour of peacock feathers through the lake. Even here the air was still loud with bird sound and it made Alicia sad, distantly sad, like she had no right to be feeling that particular kind of pain. She knew the boy was looking at the girls on the shoreline, milky and phosphorescent as they telescoped in and out of view, but it was okay somehow, just a confirmation that there were things you could always count on to be true.

'Back home,' Alicia told the boy, 'there'd be some rule saying you couldn't sell living things on the sidewalk like that.'

'What?'

'The birds.'

'It's ok here. It's tradition.'

'It's barbaric. And it's kind of creepy. You know, like Hitchcock.'

'But *Sagra dei Osei* is about singing, not dying.'

'Someone needs to tell the birds that.'

She had offended him now. They kicked along the shoreline without speaking and then the boy asked if she needed to get back to the hotel any time soon.

'Tell *me*,' she tried instead. 'About the singing,'—because it was the only connection she could make, a stepping into some dark, shared undertow of bird-haunted streets, where for centuries men had travelled hundreds of miles to market, sparrows and nightingales peddled for the magic of their song. In a way she really did want to know. It was horrific and it was sublime. It was both things and it seemed that when he took her hand to guide her off the beach along dusty, light-stippled paths of olive, and told her about how in Sacile, the oldest of the markets, a thrush would be crowned king of all songbirds, what he was really saying was that the more beautiful something could be, the closer to death it came.

'You don't find birds creepy?' she asked. 'They freak me out. Maybe it's because they're so prehistoric. And they have such quick little eyes, like their thoughts are way ahead of me.'

But it didn't translate despite her mime, or if it did it came out as something else that sounded mean when she meant it to be kind of funny, and if not funny then at least self-deprecating, like acknowledging maybe the birds were going to get the last laugh after all. Even if it was just the language barrier it made Alicia think about what Victor Minchin had said right before she told him she was going to Europe for the summer, the thing about how ironic it was that for a nerd she was so inarticulate when she opened her mouth. Except this was not the real irony, which lay in how he said *dumb* and not *inarticulate* and also how Victor Minchin explored it so inexpertly, her mouth, how he was curious but faltered, how cautiously he moved, like a prince stepping softly inside a pavilion. How his own gestures were so incapable of answering her questions. How he really had no idea what he was doing but kept on doing it anyway, which was maybe what the woman on the pedalo had felt when she rented it that morning, *I don't know what I'm doing, but this is supposed to be fun and everyone does it*, and maybe there had also been a moment, a luminous, shocking moment before the cold of the water started to compress her thinking where the woman on the pedalo had felt something new, *I should never have done this, I had no idea this could happen*, the way Alicia herself had thought this, the way she had thought, *I had no idea this could happen* even though it was the most obvious thing, the only thing that was going to happen the minute Victor Minchin told her she was dumb and she touched her hands to his face.

'Here is good,' she said.

Here was a small patch of scrub grass under the trees. Lizards basked and the heat from the sun made them slip in and out of each other's hands as they scrambled through the undergrowth.

'Strange things happen to people called Alice,' the boy said suddenly, catching her waist as she stumbled. 'They get lost in Wonderland, no?' he added, and she shook her head—'It's *Alicia*'—and reached up to show him the length of the 'a', *aaah*, like a doctor would make you say it, demonstrated the way the sound fell heavily from the mouth when you slipped it inside someone else's. The beer made her aggressive, and giddy, so it was less a kiss than an anchoring, or a taking, an act of piracy, but still it was a way in, it was a fall, a sudden silence, or the opposite; new and shared words.

When he pressed her hands behind her head she caught a tiny scent of bird clinging to her wrist.

She guessed it would be not like it was with Victor Minchin. It would be fast and certain, which didn't make it romance, but who needed that? It would have rhythm and it would have meaning, one singular moment of meaning, like a haiku breathed against her body, and because she was still in high school it was okay to measure the formative events of life against poetry. The boy touched her closed eyelids.

'You have your mother's eyes,' he said into the place where Alicia's barrette pulled hair high above her ears.

'What?'

'Beautiful. Like the sea. Like emeralds.'

'Telling me I look like my Mom is not a compliment.'

'Very beautiful,' he repeated.

'And how do you even know,' Alicia asked, kissing him back, pulling him in by the belt, 'what colour my Mom's eyes are?'

Her mother's eyes, are in fact, short-sighted, green because of genetic mutations, not magic; the myths say that the green-eyed are better at holding down long term relationships, but the myths are wrong. Rarer than gold, Alicia knows that not until the Moors invaded Spain did green eyes appear in Europe. They are the eyes of nomads and explorers or faeries and evil spirits, if you read Wikipedia. She herself has stared into a mirror, hoping to cast some kind of spell over her body, hoping that really she might be a witch after all and could undo this thing, just with her eyes. Because Alicia has a secret, a secret that has been growing in her since before she got on the plane at Newark, something that will not sink down and stay hidden no matter how many desperate prayers she invents, something she cannot tell her mother, who hasn't enough time, despite being on vacation, to wonder what her only daughter has been doing all day, or any day for that matter. Something that she is never going to tell Victor Minchin, who doesn't even understand irony and is not somebody she wants to be connected to for the rest of her life.

'Alice,' the boy is saying, out of breath. 'What are you doing? We just kiss, yes?'

'Why would we just kiss?'

'Because you are a kid, Alice!'

'Oh,' she says, wondering when it was that he realised.

She wants the feeling to come back, of the boy watching her on the hotel balcony, her white skirt billowing and rising in the evening breeze while her mother, in shadow on the other side of the floating drapes, slams and curses about the gently sweltering room. Or another feeling, of being in Victor Minchin's bedroom, right after she picked up her study notes off his bed but before they fell across the rug, before the careful, colour-coded order she'd filed them in became something else that could only happen in the past. But she cannot find either memory. It's like they don't belong to her any more. It's as though she has held the feelings in her hand and gently, and in slow-motion, brought them to her lips and blown them out. Alicia remembers now the time she met the boy in the corridor outside their room, the time when he didn't notice her, how he smelled of sweat and flowers, the translucent taut-silk shine of the skin across his back when he bent to re-tie his shoes. It is like a new pulse inside her. She lets her fingers move under his shirt, run along his spine as if it is her piano, as if she can play the memory away.

'Alice,' the boy gasps. 'This is a bad idea.'

Behind the trees the girls swim slow, labyrinthine circles through the blue, the lake water like a magnet pulling at the iron firmness of their limbs. And then they stop.

The sound of her voice—it is two things at once. Her voice is raw, like it is coming from another person's mouth, but also more her own than it has ever been. Mostly the sounds have no definition. Sometimes they could be the word *please*. It might be what it feels like to drown. Not water but too much life, crushing you.

She is aware of the girls returning to shore, suddenly, like stars into an evening sky, but truthfully Alicia has forgotten about the *Polizia di Stato* who are beginning to arrive further down the beach where the missing woman's family make terrible bargains with the universe and will time to suspend. The only thing she seems able to think of is the bird, the small, sad, wild dance of the bird on her arm, and it makes her cry the way she knows she has to cry, now that she has started this. She is crying but it feels like she is singing, like in the story of the nightingale and the rose that her father used to read, singing and singing until a thorn pierces her heart.

It's not like half the people sunning themselves on the Villa Blanca's terrace this morning didn't see the boy come to ask her go down to the promenade, didn't see how fired up he was, in such a hurry about something. It's not like there isn't a photograph somewhere in the camera of a woman called Grace, an ugly composition of dying lovebirds framing a dirty tank of fish and a local boy with his hand at the back of a young girl, sweeping her along with some kind of ardent fury. The duty officer is going to note both Alicia's evident intoxication and her date of birth in readiness for the incident report. So it doesn't matter if he didn't. Didn't. It just means that now when her mother finds out—it won't be her fault. The boy is the hotel bellhop, luggage carrier, pool cleaner; Alicia is a paying guest, an honour roll student, vacationing in Italy to improve her language skills, or at least that was the official reason her mother gave the neighbours. Those are just the facts, so. Victor Minchin would want it this way, if he knew.

The things that aren't facts don't seem to have anything to do with her any more. Suddenly they feel a very long way off, as if Alicia has never seen them before. Or maybe she has, but they looked different then. The important thing is that the way the story is written down later Alicia is not the one who rolled the boy, who is in fact twenty-two and an anthropology student at Venice International University, on top of her, and that the hands at the boy's fly are his own. That is the important thing. The important thing, and this she is sure of, is that when her mother arrives at the *Stazione di Polizia* with the Villa Blanca's manager later that evening, she needs to be sobbing fiercely in the evidence room, ready to put on record what from now on she is going to call everything.

Everything beautiful is far away

One night there was a man in the lobby who said he had come all the way from the Isle of Man to visit his wife; this was the only hospital that could treat her cancer. The only one? Really? Well no, there were others, he said. But here they could do things that would give her months and not weeks. Wasn't that worth the trip? I am not the kind of person to answer strangers. I mean, I really didn't know.

We watched the revolving doors instead of talking to each other, wondering who had it worst: the doctors who knew everything, going outside for a smoke, or the mothers who knew nothing, stubbing their cigarettes out on the wall as they ran in. I wondered this. The man in the lobby was probably thinking of other things. If I had to guess, if I was made to, I would say that weeks might be better, but that is because I am an impatient kind of person, and there is only so much anyone can bear. You go through life wanting time to speed up so you can be old enough to drive, or date a man without asking your mother's permission. You just want someone to take you seriously. You don't want anything to be measured in periods longer than weeks. What I'm really saying is that I could never be a doctor. There might be miracles but still you have the feeling everyone is bracing themselves for something else. That thing is *afterwards*. There are not enough miracles in the world to compensate for that.

I was watching the revolving doors like we were in an old Western, like this was the O.K. Corral and any minute now we were going to have to dodge the spray of fire. If I could count to ten before they opened again, I would stand up and leave. I was on seven when the man in the lobby said; I have to go up and give her a sponge bath now. They want me to have an active role in her care. Do they make you do that?

They don't. I have made it quite clear from the start what I am and am not prepared to do.

Outside the hospital there are fields, wheat I think because historically this is bread-making country. You still see windmills when you drive out over the Fen, but they don't work except on public holidays, when people come from all over to make bread as a way of bringing the past to life.

You can see the fields from any of the windows, but that is not why the windows in hospitals are there. It is not about the view. If you have ever lived by the sea you will know this. The wildness—it doesn't go away when you can't see it. I thought about the woman from the Isle of Man, how when she closed her eyes she could have the whole of the ocean if she wanted, like a long, living dream.

There is a name for the way you might want to stay in the

dream and not come back. Divers call it the rapture of the deep, but this is no more than a state of nitrous intoxication, an entirely reversible condition as long as you know to ascend to the shallows. It is not a sickness so much as not realising when you have had too much.

At night you can hear the wheat, like a song, like the sea. You hear the hum of ancient glacial planes beneath long barrows. Suddenly the surface seems very far away.

At five o'clock a nurse comes to adjust the morphine pump. This nurse, she talks to him like I never have. She touches him in a way that should make me jealous. That blue diamond inside the wrist. Poor love, she says, rubbing it to bring up the veins. Poor baby.

You notice this too when people speak to small children, or animals, how they change the tone of their voice, or make incomprehensible hand gestures. When there are no words, we forget that once the only way was touch. My sister used to say, when she was *la la*-ing nursery rhymes late into the night with Anna, well it can only ever help to try. It would take so long some nights, my sister putting Anna in the rugby ball position and swaying from side to side saying, *there there baby, la la*, a thousand times. At the worst of it I might think, *for the love of God Anna*! or I might come in and take over, it depended on how things were with my sister, if I felt sorry for her or if she had brought up the thing about the money I borrowed from our parents again. But if I did go in, there was something I knew for certain, and that was that Anna would stop crying. She'd just stop and the triumph would be all mine, which you would think I would feel good about. But all it did was make my sister feel as though she had failed in the most basic biological way. My sister would have preferred the crying to that. So on the nights I felt sorry for her, what I did was put the pillow over my head and go back to sleep.

I wanted to say to the man in the lobby, let the nurses do the sponge bath: let it go. Only my sister would know how this feels.

To start with you talk about everything. Arguments are not off limits either. Then there are the things which ordinarily wouldn't be funny enough to mention, but it turns out not so many things happen in a day, or even a week; you can't be picky. I ask him if he remembers when we went to Starcross. We drove all the way along the coast of what they call the English Riviera, where palm trees grow next to signs for fish and chips. You know, I say, I wore that patchwork skirt. You hated it because it made me look like a hippie. There were owls flying over the beach even though it was daylight. There was this sign, on the wall of the harbour, *Shellfish eaten from these waters must be boiled continuously for three minutes*. I talk fast. I talk like there is a stopwatch running and any minute someone is going to shout Stop!

His eyes are slow to open so there is time. I think of granite rubbing the back of my knees, the bright bliss of clouds: you remember things like this at the oddest of times. My hands like flat stones, splayed out behind me, the weight of the sun, which is the weight of a universe. I was a hippie back then, it's true, my hat had a sunflower stitched to the brim and I even braided my hair. I say I braided it; my sister did it for me each morning. When we went to Starcross I had to leave the braids in, night after night, until the elastic bands became part of my hair, and then my hair became elastic, I could actually stretch it right round the back of my head and still suck on the end of it. But I cut it the next year. That was the last summer I had long hair.

He nods at me, yes, sure I remember. But, he says, an owl flying in the day is not particularly unusual. Later I realise he doesn't remember at all. He can't, because he was not the one who took me to Starcross; it was another man I loved. The guilt rushes through me like my heart is a barrage, just trembling to let go. But I hold it back. I feel it, everything, all of it, like a giant lake, like the Nile behind my heart, dammed, and if anything, I am too alive.

I read him poetry, sometimes. *I stand in another world*, I read. *Not the past, not the future.*

He says, 'You want to get further away than that'.

Mostly I read to him from my magazines. I tell him about the rugby player who has just come out of the closet.

'Let him fuck whom he wants', he says.

'Who he wants', I say. 'Who'.

But suddenly I am not sure of anything at all, even grammar.

They don't provide meals for visitors, even regular ones, but we have struck a deal with the Thai orderly who brings the food. He is fed through a naso-gastric tube, but we fill in a menu for him anyway and the Thai orderly says nothing as long as I give him last week's *Hello* magazine and rub his arse as he leaves. Not everyone thinks hospital food is worth this kind of subterfuge but I was a child of the Eighties. If it didn't come out of a box, a packet or a boilable plastic bag I didn't eat.

The coffee is terrible though.

In the concourse I see the man from the lobby, which gives me the sudden urge to buy him a latte. Maybe it is just because he is familiar and all. It is late, but I think I might want to tell him something. His eyes seem far away. He says, 'Damn fine coffee', to which I answer, 'And hot!' which shows both our age and a mutual preference for surreal and morally questionable drama. But we both know it is not true. The coffee is bitter and scalds our palates. He keeps sipping, and I want to ask him if it's possible it isn't the coffee but the words, the ones neither of us are saying, that are responsible for this.

Someone has left a newspaper on the table, open at a page that chronicles the history of the search for extra-terrestrial life. We haven't got very far in fifty years, it turns out. The waitress shouts, Closing! and the noise of the security grille descending drowns out the section I start to read aloud.

'Do you think', the man from the lobby says later, 'it would be worse if it turned out we are alone in the universe after all?'

❧

Across town from the hospital is a hotel building made entirely of glass. This is where I go when it is time to leave the ward. I tell him I am going and he raises a hand in a slow salute. Even at the last minute I turn. Like Orpheus, like Lot's wife, like every TV movie ever made. If I were in a TV movie I would say his name as a question when I turned. Our gaze would be capable of penetrating vast distances, as if our eyes were meeting across a lake. And then I would say, quietly; 'Nothing.'

It takes forty-five minutes to walk through the city. You could do it in a cab in less than ten, but if you have never run away from anything then you will not know what it is to need the power of your own limbs.

The city at night is submarine, dark, like a Caspar David Friedrich. I paddle downstream. I slip in and out of streets like they are bays and I am a boat, nudging into harbour. Any floating vessel will do; the Jumblies went to sea in a sieve. I cast out and sail into the centre of the moonlit city and I wear the silence like a fur. All about my feet I see the stars and I am treading on the stars. With just my feet I kick whole constellations into touch.

The foyer is like any regular hotel foyer except you can look out of every wall, and anyone can look in. Even the darkness is transparent. I think, this is what fish must see in an aquarium. I move through corridors into other worlds, luminous in the depths, followed by the scent of salt and death.

Perhaps I will not forgive him for what he said about the

owls. There are subtler ways of communicating anger than I ever knew.

Underneath the man from the lobby I at least have the decency not to move. His weight like water. My blood like a foreign tide.

Now whenever I am in a tall building the urge to jump is reverent.

We went to marriage counselling a few times, which some people find surprising and to this I say: illness doesn't make you a saint. Anger is the real problem for us both. The counsellor says that very often it is not the loss of an actual thing that makes us angry but all the potential things. This was a long time ago and it was in response to his complaint that I never do the washing up, which we learned—I learned—is not about good domestic hygiene but respect. When you are fighting over the dirty coffee cups you are really saying, *love me*. But now I understand what it is the counsellor actually meant.

Suddenly it becomes very important to have tried scuba diving. Suddenly it becomes important to have eaten shellfish that have not been boiled continuously for at least three minutes, or to fuck *whom* you want. Knowledge becomes the important thing. I have never been to the circus so I cannot say for sure why it is exploitative of animals. I have so little right to take part in so many debates.

Suddenly it becomes very important to have been in love, truly in love, the kind that could cross continents and survive the darkest histories, made deeper by its own wounds. Who doesn't want to love that way? I want to say to the counsellor; really, find me someone who doesn't want to love that way.

This is something I would show you if I could. To understand, you need to know that there is a stone plaque above the reception desk in the hospital lobby, carved to look as if it is really old. But you can tell it isn't because of the shape of the letter 's'. The plaque says *Whatever it is, it will pass*. And what you think is, yes—but when?

There is a woman in this city whose name I will never know so I imagine her as Bella, which was the name of my first dog. The woman might not even be from the city. People come to this hospital from all over the world. Our eyes meet in the mirror of the bathroom in nuclear medicine. 'You too?' she says.

I say nothing. I am dispensing soap. I don't even know what she means. Me? Then I understand yes, she means me, there is no-one else here. I run my hands over the warm tap to rinse them, but it feels so good I hold them there another minute. The water starts to steam and hurt but I don't take my hands away. I know her look; I have worn it myself. I want to say it is hopeful, but the word I really want is famished.

'It will pass', she says.

The sting of my hands? No.

'But what if it doesn't?' I ask, and I can see she has never thought of that.

In the mirror my shape is feral. I have crow's feet. I look

out of them but they are not my eyes. I look up and what I see is not the ceiling but a closed lid. They say fluorescent light is the most unflattering kind but in it what I feel is savage, and not myself. This is just flattery in disguise. What else is flattery but telling you that you look like something you are not, to make you feel better about the thing that you are.

The hospital soap is called Hibiscrub, which might refer to the inhibiting of bacteria, but the overwhelming perfume says to me, *hibiscus*. A delicacy in Mexico; the national flower of Malaysia. Tahitian women wear a single red hibiscus behind their ear to show they are ready to be a wife. In the mirror crimson petals bloom violently against my cheek. The last thing I want to smell of is flowers. I run my hands under the tap, rubbing hard on the back and front the way the surgeons do. I hook right in under the nails. The door bangs shut behind the woman I call Bella but I do not stop scrubbing. I might have been doing it for half an hour, it might be I am there all day. This is what I want to show you: it doesn't pass.

One night I tell him I want to get fish and chips. There is only so much rehydrated food anyone can eat without compromising the basic human desire to stay alive. He raises his hand as I leave the room. He says, 'pass me the mirror, I want to do my hair.' Then he says, 'I liked it when you were a hippie'. I say, 'you didn't know me when I was a hippie'. But then I turn. I say his name, like a question.

I sit in the patients' lounge, in the dark. I pull the vertical blinds and listen to the winter wind, coming in from far away. It has never frightened me like it does some people. I try to imagine what it is to be far away and realise this; that I am too close.

What I realise is that everything beautiful is far away.

I catch the bus home and then I take the car that has been sitting in the garage these past seven months and drive half way across the country to Starcross. Around Birmingham I realise I have left my phone in his bedside locker, along with the book I am reading and my hairbrush.

I start to think in threes, as if what I can see in front of me is not the slope of the motorway but just the beginning, the middle and an end.

There is no colour along the coast apart from the sea pinks, brave in what is still moonlight. Winds hit heavy against the groynes. The air that blows in the window smells of tanker oil and the radio plays a cover version of The Smiths song, *Please Please Please* let me get what I want. The piano rises and I listen, and I think: but how can you get what you want if you don't know what that is?

By morning the sky and the waves are the same, smashing down against the sand which looks like snow, which all along the edge of the world is as fine as snow.

I lied about what I said when I left his room. But I cannot repeat them again, the words I used.

The other man I loved had black hair, like Leonard Cohen's gypsy boy. Who am I to presume he felt anything in return? I think of the song, *Scarborough Fair*, and I wonder if he remembers me at all. There are times when it seems more than I can do to remember how to breathe and suddenly everything I have ever known is gusting back to me, dredged through the stink of tanker oil from an old place at the bottom of my heart. Suddenly it feels as if the seventy-eight per cent of my body that is water is trying to get back to the sea. *Sehnsucht*, the Germans call this. An intense yearning for a thing far-off, a thing that no word in the English language can define.

A gull flies out of the surf and taps down lightly on the sand; then another. But, miraged behind the spray, it is possible it is just the same bird. When I reach Starcross the shellfish sign is still there on the harbour wall and it's been fifteen years.

Even at this hour there is a man selling chips from a truck stand. I am like one of those crazy people who will talk to anyone. I tell the vendor about the rugby player who has come out of the closet. He hands me my food. He doesn't look like a person who cares.

On the other side of the wall the water shudders in, the visible surface tremor of an innately rocking world. A bottle smacks the stone, eddies down and goes under. Today the sea is a breathing sheet of lead. The entire sea is a stone, shattering. I am out of metaphors. The sea is just the sea. This is the Earth. In space we are just the remnants of ancient, accidental collisions. But this doesn't explain our longing, or desire. It is obscene, if you think about it, the way we take so long to realise anything.

Here is one way to look at it. It is like the shock of realising that nothing is new, that you—still so resiliently un-clonable—are not new. I don't mean this in any zen kind of way, I mean it the way it sounds. Sometimes you can think that you were the one to discover something only to find out that everybody knew about it all along. It is always a shock to learn that other people have been in the same place as you.

There is a pencil on my desk that says 'I used to be a Paper cup!' in black stencilled letters down the side. I know this is possible, that we can recycle anything, but still I find myself holding my pencil in wonder, and crying.

❧

If people ask I will tell them it was peaceful. But how can any of us know this?

I eat my chips. I wave down to the beach as if there is somebody out there who will realise it is me. I call my own name, just to hear it aloud, just to allow it to enter, for a moment, a different world.

Not the past, not the future. Not paradise not reality not a dream.

It is only last week I read him that poem.

Here is something else I do not know. If it passes—what then?

Note: The poem quoted by the narrator is *Wildly Constant* by Anne Carson, from *The Forward Book of Poetry 2010*, Forward London, 2009.

The smallest of things

The woman on the bus had done her laundry the day before. Or Monday, perhaps. There were two loads of colours and then the whites, so possibly she had been washing over two days. When she thought about it, the woman on the bus had in fact washed a fourth load too because yesterday was the day they changed the sheets. The problem with the tumble dryer meant that they had to delay one load, so laundry was almost certainly what she had been doing for the last two days. It was unacceptable that no engineers were available over the holiday weekend because this had an impact on how many loads you could expect to get through in a day, and you would hope for a contingency plan at least, because even on public holidays the laundry had to be done.

The woman on the bus had recently been to a local beauty spot, where the parking charges were also unacceptable and there was only one four-hourly tariff, although they had still chosen to use the facility. It turned out the beauty spot was really only somewhere beautiful, which seemed not to be what the woman on the bus was expecting, so they stayed just an hour, which gave them a surplus of parking time. A family pulled up in a nearby space and the woman on the bus asked if they would like the unused portion of the ticket. But the young wife, who had moon-shaped hollows under her eyes and a stain on her liberty print dress, said yes so sharply—*Yes!*—that it made the woman on the bus not want to give it to her any more.

It was almost certainly a completely unrelated action but the driver pulled up particularly hard then and we all learned that the woman on the bus had a *spiky knee*, although we had no frame of reference for this condition, which might have represented some external expression of an inner angst, or been slang for something degenerative and related to shitty bones. There was no way of telling whether the information was meant as a threat, but the man standing in the wheelchair bay took it seriously enough to risk moving into the aisle, notoriously vulnerable to the ricochet effect at the point the bus hit the car traps, which was the part you had to brace yourself for even though the whole guided busway project had cost the taxpayer millions and was advanced in other, more invisible ways.

Even though it was traditionally the way things were done, the woman on the bus had no intention of thanking the bus driver at her destination. The woman on the bus felt that, seeing as his driving was intolerable and there were not enough seats, thanking him would be in some way a betrayal of her core beliefs, which her therapist had encouraged her to preserve. The lack of seats was not in itself the responsibility of the driver but the woman on the bus had little doubt it was made worse by his poor judgment calls, mostly relating to where there was a line of international students waiting at the local college, which was a point that closed the debate almost immediately because it involved discussion of immigration and political allegiances that some people preferred not to talk about on the bus. There was a moment at which a girl on a bicycle had made an ill-judged attempt to cross the bus rails and the driver was forced to lurch to a halt, but this was a regular occurrence and no-one's heart had stopped, no-one's life flashed in disappointing vignettes before their eyes, which meant even the woman on the bus had to accept that the foolishness displayed was entirely the fault of the girl, although it wouldn't have hurt the driver to sound the horn.

It was also normal to expect a delay where the bus had to cross a taxi lane to make a left downtown, but the intersection was on this occasion unusually clear and provoked vocal speculation as to why the city was so quiet, which meant we never did find out if the woman on the bus gave her unused parking ticket to the young wife with the moon-hollowed eyes. The suspicion was—*not*. You couldn't quite see through the window because of all the breathing going on in the bus, but it was enough to tell it was raining, which caused a problem with the preparation of umbrellas in a small space and seemed unfair considering at the start of the journey there had been the promise of wide, clear skies and even a little sun. It was as if the bus itself had absorbed all the best things the day might have been able to offer and released them back to the world in the form of a very fine, very intrusive vapour, the kind that your clothes would take in and slowly discharge at inopportune intervals throughout the morning, like you were breathing water, like a reminder we shouldn't have left the ocean.

The woman on the bus expressed an opinion that implied this change in the weather was also the fault of the driver, albeit in some way that couldn't quite be qualified. Perhaps if he had driven more slowly. Perhaps if he had been someone else. The implication seemed to be that had he driven more slowly or been a different person we might have arrived in the city at some other point in the space-time continuum, some point where it was not raining and we did not have to contemplate the evolutionary processes that had made us so incompatible with our environments, shaped us into such exposed, susceptible forms and then failed us. The sky was momentarily pale gold and still, and for a minute we wondered if this was possible, if so much could really be so different based on a change in the smallest of things. Then the rain returned, firm and regular, and equally it seemed inevitable that all paths were fixed and you were going to wind up in the same place eventually, anyway.

The woman on the bus had another stop to sit out all the lurching and ricocheting. We disembarked at New Square, the stop that was easy to miss since they renamed it with a generic indication that you were in the city now but not precisely where, not on *exactly which street*, uncertain as we departed whether our mumbled gratitude to the driver was an act of treachery or defiance.

The old madness and the sea

Murray had never been afraid to call a spade a spade. A rose is a rose is a rose Gina had said. But it meant the same thing, or at least, that was what he assumed. She told him she was a widow and he'd been prepared to believe it, but he didn't take it for granted. He had never seen any photographs of a husband or family but then, neither did he carry a picture of his wife in his wallet. So it meant nothing either way. All he knew was that when he was with her he felt capable of a motion fluid and unstoppable, as if she were a delta and he the river flooding into her, and Murray didn't want to stop too long to think about anything that might slow the movement down. He was an unremarkable man, and the thought of being an analogy was about as exciting as anything else that had happened to him in recent months. He had never considered himself to be in any way talented and suddenly here were two things he had discovered a gift for: telling a lie and getting away with it. It was hard to tell if that was a consequence of something else or if the capacity for it had always been there like an old cup or a fossilised bone, just waiting in the regolith of the earth to be exposed. He guessed a little of both. Yeah, that's right, he wanted to tell Hazel. I know words like regolith.

He worked for a company that installed satellite television. A good majority of people who ordered some kind of mini-dish system made an impromptu decision at a supermarket or after reading a flyer in a lifestyle magazine, but when he started back after his second tour they sent him out on the door to door rota, where, divorced from an already cranked up, reckless need to spend, it was harder to convince people they wanted what he had to sell. And on the one hand that was a good thing because what Murray needed immediately was a routine challenge, although what he needed long term was something different, something that could alleviate that feeling of being caught in midstream, like an eel lost on unknown currents in its return to the Sargasso.

She lived on a street where the backs of the houses faced the sea but the fronts looked out onto an identical, faintly municipal terrace separated from the road by iron railings. Immediately Murray liked the illusion, the delay of the moment in which the sea revealed itself as some sort of magician's trick. He had not looked at her face when she opened the door but away over her shoulder to the French windows and the bay beyond, saw the water vital and molten beyond the glass and made some sort of involuntary noise that didn't even come close to being a word. She seemed appreciative. He struggled to reel off the standard lines, the request for just a minute of her time.

'Normally I wouldn't,' she told him. 'But as it happens,

today I'm feeling rash.' So he followed her inside, product information at the ready, with the trepidation of a fire-eater who knows his craft inside out but fears his knowledge will one day fail and burn him.

Everything about the room was geared up to an appreciation of the sea. The sky seemed a high mirror, brilliant and backlit. Even the light was tidal. As Murray stood there looking it seemed the sky and the clouds were in a constant bid to change places with each other and for no good reason he remembered lying on his back on hot white sand with a girl he'd once known who said that all things emerged from the sea only to spend their whole life longing to return to it.

He had few words to offer and none of them involved satellite television. 'The sea's pretty,' was the best he could manage, in the first instance. She stared at him with an amused twist of her mouth. 'Yes,' she said. 'It does look pretty good from here.'

Murray had never previously engaged in shameless flirting and responded with a little flourish of his document case that he immediately regretted.

'How about getting down to business,' he said and then regretted that too. It happened, sometimes, that women—and it was often the divorcees but he didn't want to generalise—would come on to him a little and he would shake it off, maybe throw in a joke or two just to keep the mood sweet and more often than not, a deal closed; there was something about signing a direct debit mandate that made these women quick to bare their soul. He wanted to tell her that she didn't need what he was trying to sell, that staring at a screen all day robbed you of your thoughts and God knows, that was all you did, once you gave in and signed up, whatever anybody said about all those documentary channels being educational. But the living room wall was a lattice of books and he saw how the geometry of the water beyond the window cut strong, dazzling lines across the room, over the furniture and the two people standing in its luminous sweep, and looking into her bright face he could tell that she already knew better and whatever being rash meant, it did not mean subscribing to satellite television. She was older than Hazel and Murray had the ridiculous thought that of the two, this woman standing in front of him now was the more real, as if she were part of the sun and the water and Hazel was merely a reflection, a thought, temporary. He shook it off. Sat on the sofa, accepted the offer of coffee, got up again and walked back over to the window. Touched the bookshelves, disturbed the deep quadrants of light.

'I had a friend who left a man because he hadn't read D.H. Lawrence,' she said.

When he turned around she was holding a mug of coffee, offering it out like a gift. He looked down to see his hand resting on *Women in Love* and guilty, Murray picked it up, thumbed idly from a scribbled message on the inside front cover to about half way through. 'I've not read very much Lawrence,' he said, apologetic.

'Lady Chatterley?'

'Yes.'

'You just read the dirty bits?'

'Yes.'

'The folded warmth,' she said, in what he supposed was

meant to be a northern accent. 'The secret entrances. Tha's got the nicest arse of anybody.'

He was embarrassed to see himself in the mirror opposite, his face flushed an adolescent rosacea, the document case resting, protectively, against him in a manner that reminded him of being at school. He tried to think of what the Bank of England was supposed to be doing to interest rates, the crack in Azaria's bedroom ceiling that might indicate subsidence, tulips. If it hadn't been for the name badge hanging around his neck he would have had trouble recognising himself. The suit was particularly incongruous. Squinting, Murray saw a different outline, one wearing DPMs and a Shemagh, and suddenly he wished this woman could also see him like that, dark and dusty and alive, like Lawrence of Arabia. But she was treated only to this version of him, informed, predictable, the version that Hazel positively encouraged and tried to take with her to barbecues and National Childbirth Trust benefits.

He was about to speak, but she got there first, seeing his face.

'I'm sorry,' she said. 'That was inappropriate. Sit down. I'm quoting, obviously.'

He should have left, or breathed a sigh of relief, but as soon as he didn't Murray stepped into a different pool, one into which pretty much every other person he worked with had already dipped a toe and either basked or drowned, and one which suddenly he felt was his due.

In the quake of his grip against the wall she was reproachful. 'You haven't even asked my name,' she said and for a minute he didn't want to know, understanding that anonymity was like an armour and it was his responsibility to keep it shining. Still, there was an inscription on the inside of *Women in Love* and he couldn't help whispering Gina, Gina, *Gina*, and as he said it, tipping her head as if to drink from her, kissing her full on the lips and then again in the pale valley beneath her ear, he felt the balance of her tension change as if he had unlocked her and dislodged some fundamental possibility, one where maybe love could come like this, at first sight and without asking. And he would have believed this, except his breathing synchronised with the heave of the sea outside and fucking her was just the relief of some submarine urge, not anything to do with love at all.

Murray didn't feel very much to blame, if he was honest. He felt sudden gusts of entitlement to infidelity. He was no more than an aimless moon orbiting within a bigger system that made cheating possible, where no-one could afford to get the work they really wanted so you took what you could get and it meant you had to travel and you were permanently angry, and it was so easy to be able to say you had to stay at a motel because it made no sense to drive all the way home at the end of a long day. Yes, he said to Hazel, it was the company's expense and no, he hadn't really got a choice: these were not the right economic times in which to complain. To add to the veneer of authenticity he threw in an anecdote about having overheard a French girl talking on her mobile about *le credit crunch* when he was getting fuel. So there's no translation, he said. That's funny. And Hazel, who did not want to sound possessive, agreed that it was funny and reminded him that Azaria had her appointment with the paediatrician upcountry at the end of the week. She didn't have to add that he should be there and he wondered again about that word *imperative* and why it was he had heard it so many times since his daughter was born.

Wasn't that the dingo baby's name? someone asked him once, but he was too young to remember that. Hazel chose it, was his stock response. It was unusual but he still didn't know if he liked it, which made him feel bad, as if he was letting his daughter down just by having no opinion of what they had christened her. He had opinions of so few of the things they were supposed to share, he was beginning to realise. Some time the year before, Azaria had been to a party and the birthday girl's mother had transferred a small, temporary tattoo onto the back of her hand. Predictably the appeal had rapidly waned and as Murray sat washing the tattoo away, patiently rubbing the soap into Azaria stroke by stroke, he wondered when he would feel the magic, when all this would become more than just washing ink off someone else's skin and an experience that changed him from the core outwards.

He supposed it probably already had, but in ways that couldn't be audited. When he phoned home, hearing Azaria's breathy garble about school and friends, the way her sentences broke as the signal faded in and out and he had to make up what she was trying to tell him; those might have been the moments. He asked Hazel what was up and she told him little things, like the cat had brought in another vole and they were both coming down with something, summer flu maybe. Oh, and Azaria had written a poem that got a special recognition from the headmistress. 'Listen to this,' Hazel said. 'I hated it when I saw a potato, but I loved it when I saw a swan.' Murray sat in the car, windows down, dropping into a daze where all he could hear were the waves bashing at the seaweed line like a military battery, out of sight behind the dunes, but he told Hazel he loved it too, and she said she missed him and was proud of all the work he was doing, how hard he worked for the family.

He switched off his phone, made to walk back out into the warm night. He had no idea what the hell it even meant. I hated it when I saw a potato? For just a minute he stopped to crush a pinch of midges against the car window, picturing his wife making dinner, cutting vegetables and dancing, the superlative twist of her hip that always prompted their little joke: Hazel, you're nuts. And then the midges were gone, part of the skin of his fingertips, part of him, and the feeling vanished, which meant he was just a man alone in the white moonlight with the sea roaring.

It was a simpler pleasure, lying under Gina's coverlet looking up the light, marvelling at the way you could still see it through the cotton, diffuse and spluttering. At least once a week he would show up at her door and she would have him come in, make him coffee and they pretended it meant absolutely nothing, that she was still thinking about the different deals and whether a Film or a Sports package was the more appropriate way to go. He fell asleep to soft and repeated explosions of rain. Morning after morning he woke up to the pulse of hidden waves.

Murray hadn't smoked since college but he didn't say no when she offered him a joint, waving off the apology that it was poor quality, just the stalks that no-one wanted. There was a balcony that led off the main bedroom to look directly out onto the bay, and standing on it, stretching into the wind, he wondered what you did with a surfeit of beauty, like really, what could you do with it, and if he had to explain it to Hazel, would she understand that when others in his command had craved sex, a decent steak, all he had longed he for in the desert was the simplicity of rain. He wondered if this behaviour was the result of their inability to give that to each other: simplicity. Of them not having the money to buy this kind of life where all you had to do was get out of bed and look out onto the end of the land, the lights of the deep water, its animalistic seethe, where there was a chance that the velocity of the waves could cancel out a person's own internal surge. But that didn't seem fair, to hold this against her. The entire ocean. Their landlocked existence. Fuck, he thought, pitching the joint down towards the purple sand below. This is so fucked up.

Standing beside the bed, he looked at Gina's face and although it made him happy to see her smile up at him, he saw also that something in its illumination was not just for him, and he remembered the time, visiting a cathedral somewhere down South, when he had stood in the coloured pool of a stained glass window, marvelling at the way it liquefied stone, his own skin even, until he turned and saw others behind him, caught up in the same, tired marvel.

'Are you okay?' she said. 'You don't look okay.'

'No, no,' he said, climbing in. 'This is perfect.'

❧

Some habits must have been persistent because once she asked him if he had been in the army. He shook his head. 'Territorial,' he said, like it made a difference.

'Oh,' she said. 'When they did that Shock and Awe stuff on Baghdad, I have to tell you I felt ashamed.'

He didn't say anything. He didn't like to speak of it much, failing to see the point in talking as therapy. Too often he felt fraudulent in his trauma, knowing he had not experienced anything like what could be described as the worst. He had a scar from shoulder to elbow on the inside and of course she was going to ask about it. The ridge of torn skin shone like a streak of paraffin wax; touching it reminded her of the sensation of handling cotton wool, which had always made her gag. 'Oh, that,' he said. 'Wasn't anything much.' It wasn't. He had caught himself on the door of an armoured vehicle, which had been embarrassing more than it was painful. But he resented how the mistake had altered the topography of his body in such a misleading way.

Before he sold satellite dishes, before Azaria, before Iraq, Murray had been a printer and his hands still released the sharp odour of ink when clapping or making any sudden, close movement. At inappropriate times the fume of the press would explode from him, turpentine, pitch resin, carbon, peach, the ink liquor contradicting other smells buried deep in his palms that gave him away, even if he didn't realise it. More than once Gina reached for him and caught instead the scent of lavender handcream, and that was okay with her. It was just the two of them in the dark, where his skin was phosphorescent and she was happy to pretend it glowed just for her.

❧

Still. Closer they drew to fairytales.

About two months in there was a night storm. Murray had already thought it was a bad idea to get high on a balcony but there was something in the violence of water on water. She made mojitos and carried them out on a tray, flipping her skirt at him in time to the music from a stereo indoors. Her body tried to rest against his, leaning in as if they were in their own parenthetical world, but he shrugged her off, standing straight to watch some fireworks on the other side of the bay.

Here's something, he heard himself saying. As it flows into Mesopotamia, the Tigris draws close to the bank of the Euphrates like a twin. Bridges bind the two rivers like an ancient spine. This is where the written alphabet was invented, where words were sent out into the waters to flow down to the cities, flooding the *khans* and the *suqs* until they emptied themselves into the sea, where they scattered and civilised the world. Words that flowed from the nation between the rivers.

It felt like something he might have read in a book; it was not his voice, although he believed it. 'Gina,' he said. 'Isn't it sad what we've done? Gina?' But the rum was beginning to bite and in his head he had already moved on, wasn't thinking about the Tigris or the Euphrates any more.

'You know, my name isn't Gina,' she said, pushing the paper umbrella to one side of the glass as she sipped.

'It's not?' He was a little stunned. 'Then what's the name in the book?'

'I don't know. Which book? I pick most of them up in charity shops.'

He tried to remember back to seeing the name in *Women in Love* that first time. 'Why didn't you say?' he demanded and she just shrugged.

'I guess I quite liked it. I don't know when we're going to start being honest with each other, but I thought it might be handy if your wife comes looking for me. Nobody round here is going to know a Gina.'

On the other side of the bay smoke drifted in lazy parachutes, rising and falling with the somnambulant motion of jellyfish, and Murray could only suppose she was right.

'They say that men fall in love three times,' she said accusingly. 'The first is puppy love, the second is the one you marry. The third time is the deathbed bride. Which one am I?'

He said nothing, still mesmerized by the jellyfish. But she was agitated now and he dug into his back pocket and pulled out a sweaty resin sphere.

'Slow down small pony,' he whispered into her hair. She walked inside to change the music, put on Bob Dylan's historic Halloween concert at Philharmonic Hall and he then pulled her back into the cave of his chest, letting them both disappear in the dark.

❧

She took a phone call later in the evening. When she came back to the balcony there were tears in her eyes and Murray saw it there again in her face, the sun-stripped light that made her unknown to him. 'That was my daughter,' she said. 'She just had a little boy. Oh God, I'm a grandma.'

'Jesus,' he said. He hardly knew where to look. 'Congratulations.'

'Thank you. *Thank you*. He was only dinky. Six pounds. I can't believe my baby just gave birth. Shit, that makes me feel old.'

Murray rubbed his temples, shook his head as if he had just stepped out of a swimming pool. She looked put out. 'I'm sorry,' he said, pulling his hand away. 'I'm just trying to get my head around this.'

'I guess I never mentioned my daughter, did I?' she said.

Amongst other things, he thought. He felt mildly unwell. He blundered through polite phrases. He asked if she would go to visit them.

'No, no. I don't travel.'

'You don't–?'

'Not since my husband died. I haven't left this house in, what, I guess eight years.' She crossed her legs and rearranged herself to look out across the water as if tracking some distant boat over the horizon. 'Public transport gives me the jitters. I see a rucksack unattended and—never mind. It's fine. They'll send me photographs. God bless the Internet.'

'Well this is new,' he said, lost.

They must have sat for half an hour, not talking. A jazz

of lights flew into the sky and fell back into the water like fire. He imagined it was a birthday, or a wedding, at one of the fishing villages along the coast but it looked for all the world like flares asking for help. One or other of them made another batch of mojitos. Finally, for something to say, she volunteered, 'Aren't the fireworks pretty.'

The fireworks *were* pretty. Pretty and distant like diamonds in a deep mine or something else he could describe but had never seen. The lights died down and the sky became perfect again. 'I don't know about you,' he said. 'But I for one am hungry.'

He went into the house, blind in the absence of the searing sea gleam, and made a snack out of what he could find in the refrigerator, some kind of egg fried rice with bacon and tinned sweet corn. 'They're naming him Ben,' she called from outside. 'It means precious son.' But he could hardly hear against the sound of the bacon cooking and Bob Dylan and the waves. And in the dark he enjoyed the dizziness of his high and wondered about Azaria, whose name meant blessed of God, the sort of name you would expect to find in a Dylan song, the guitars playing over it and over it. Azaria. Gitt-tar. *Gitt*-tar. An hour later he was still there, in the kitchen, spooning the last of the rice into his mouth, thinking how sweet, how painful music could be when you shouldn't be hearing it.

They woke up shy, in damp, white half-light. The clock said 4.30am and she tasted a little drunk still. He waited until she drifted off again, memorising the motion of her sleep for the time when he wouldn't know her.

Outside the morning felt clean and unfamiliar, as if he was on holiday, which in a sense he was. A paper boy curved across the junction into her road, satchel slung so low on his back it almost touched the rear wheel of his bike and Murray felt the sea all around him like a second skin. Minus the water and plus a whole lot of sand it was almost like how it had felt in the desert, when he'd wanted to be at home. Of course when he was home he wanted to be in the desert, a pressing, contradictory urgency which he imagined was how it perhaps felt to be a snake ready to shed. And most of it he was okay with but there was a boy, one boy, who he couldn't shake out of his head and he supposed he must have died on his way home from school because he was still holding an exercise book, his face perfect as if no more had happened than he had been overcome with tiredness and had just stopped to rest by the road. Except his leg was missing. Murray had never before understood what was meant by a missing leg. Missing implied that it could be found, returned, but the hole reached right up into the boy's pelvis and beyond so the lower ribs hung back down into the space like gentle white hands trying to re-sculpt what was lost.

He rubbed his nose on both sleeves, thinking about it now. The boy's leg, a total absence. As if it had never been.

The boy on the bicycle was fifteen, maybe. Azaria was barely five so his experience in assessing the ages of children was limited to pre-schoolers and he didn't like to do more than hazard a guess. Everyone looked so old from one angle, so young from another. Murray could not reconcile the idea of his own aging, feeling himself unchanged at some deep level, a level he suspected would exist even at sixty, at eighty. The regolith. He recalled a documentary where some comedian went to New Zealand and had a Samoan give him a tattoo. When Samoans tattoo their faces, he learned, they are recording marks in time. You would never cover your face in one go. The lines would be captured bit by bit until you were an old man and the stories of your life were painted on your skin, looking out. To illustrate yourself in this way could only be a beautiful thing, an art, not a monstrosity.

The engine fell into a smooth start and he shifted gears, sank his foot onto the clutch. The car smelled of warm sleeping bags and Tupperware. He switched radio channels and looked up to see a cloud of birds ascend into an almost perfect arrow before forging ahead on some unseen thermal. Swans *were* kind of cool, he thought. He liked that Azaria had identified with them in some way, though what she had against potatoes he couldn't imagine.

He heard the car screaming to a halt before he registered the boy in front of him, the bicycle wheels locked into the perpendicular, his own head mashed against the airbag. He sat for a minute, listening to his heart going. The last of the birds rose from the dawn chorus and either settled across the telegraph wires or sheeted into the sky. He couldn't think what he was doing there on that street at five am. The light poured into the bay like it was flowing through the neck of a bottle and a tiny sound came from his throat.

He had only gotten a few blocks away. He thought of the sleeping woman who was not called Gina, if she was awake yet, if she was expecting him to come back, or if she had ever really assumed that he would stay. He was wondering if going back was even possible now. The small things seemed so distant. The tight spiral of Azaria's curls; Hazel combing them.

He looked up. The boy flipped him the bird and backed off, skimmed out into the street. A caesura, broken softly.

Countdown

The thing she had, the affliction, the syndrome, was like nothing the best minds in medical science had seen before. In the foyer of A&E they lifted her like cloth sacking from my arms, gurneyed and triaged her; no she had not fallen, vomited, taken anything. Her temperature was pushing fever point, that was the most they could say. 'Do we have her notes?' the nurse wanted to know. She kept asking, even when the notes were in her hand. 'These are from geriatrics,' the nurse was shouting. And then; 'Does anyone else hear ticking?'

What I heard when I pressed my ear to Catherine's heart was the rage of memories, a shudder of years collapsing in. I picked up her hand and kissed its sudden smoothness, the tiny adolescent pearls of her nails. 'Look at this!' she said, her voice soft as fur, and we looked as she slipped from the bed, cartwheeled to the nurse's station. 'I haven't done that in years,' she said, hip-height at my side, giddy and breathless and young.

There were rumours, the specialist in experimental diagnostics said, of isolated cases like Catherine's, usually in remote areas, the places time forgot and then remembered, over-compensating. Cases of what? was all I wanted to know, watching the hours flood through her, lightning-fast.

'Was it catching? Was it curable? Can we get this place quarantined?' the specialist said looking through me to the picture window and the famous view that tourists flew for a whole day to come and see. 'And get her back in bed. Do we have any books? Puzzles? What do kids play with these days?'

I took Catherine's hand, kissed her, let whatever it was that was happening to her enter me too. 'Don't hurt me,' she said, crying, and I picked her up, rocked her in my arms, tickled her bare feet while the nurses took blood, swabs, measured the amount of time she had left. 'Tell me a story,' she said, and I told her the one about how we met, which seemed more like a fairytale than a thing in any book I'd read.

The corridors telescoped away into darkness but all I could see was Catherine, retreating. Midnight came and there was only one place to go. I took her up to the hospital roof, stared out into the wide night sky. Something to do with the clock was the theory, leaking out with every chime, every tick, every new moment, the fall-out seeping into the Thames, pulsing uptide, into estuaries, out to sea, to everyone. A pandemic, sighed the specialist, falsely stoic.

I pressed myself to Catherine's sweet baby-smell, rested my head against the place where her sternum was a bridge between her body and mine. Then I started the countdown, listened for the quiet stroke of the remaining hours in her chest.

Let it out

This is the thing that happened to you and Claudine L. two summers ago, when you were on international exchange in Buenos Aires. Your Drama and Movement Therapy year. You weren't going to talk about it, ever, but what the hell. The first thing to say is that even now you have no idea whether or not Buenos Aires looks like Paris. You think it is almost a criminal offence that your parents never took you to Paris so that you could make these comparisons for yourself. Someday you will go there and all you will be able to think is; this is like Buenos Aires. Except by then Paris will be the poor relation. It will be the blind date that never showed up leaving you to drown your sorrows with the average-looking guy at the bar. You don't actually mean that Buenos Aires is average. You mean: this is your parents' fault. By *this* you mean: everything.

Your father says Drama and Movement Therapy is not something you can study but a way of talking shit at his expense, and to this you say: he is an engineer and just doesn't understand the way the body can be healed through the creative imagination. When you think of your father you feel like a globe of ink plummeting to the bottom of a glass of water. It goes without saying that Drama and Movement therapy involves a lot of talking, a fact of which you would have no doubt been aware sooner had you signed up for your degree based on appropriate talents and not opportunities for subsidised world travel. You have recently had the delayed epiphany that your temperament is better suited to working with inanimate objects, like books or motors, but those students do not visit Latin America to learn about psychoanalysis and the therapeutic power of art. Here is an irony your father would enjoy: you are just not comfortable talking about some things.

For instance, what happened to you in Arrivals at Ministro Pistarini International Airport. Or what your father did with the Polish cleaner on your mother's Chesterfield the year before you left for college. You could have kept quiet about that, but because you wanted the neighbours' kids to like you, you leant over the fence to describe the frantic motion of your father's penis above the Polish cleaner's pale thighs in such exquisite detail that none of them could look you in the eye all holiday. It is ideologically rather inconvenient that you have reached this conclusion: sometimes not talking is the better option.

This need to be liked is something you might call a problem. Personally you are uncertain of the boundaries between *like* and *love*, although professionally you call it erotic transference and own text books telling you where to draw the line. For this reason you worry that people will think this story is just the consequence of loneliness, or drug abuse, when it was neither of those things, although you had just started to experiment with marijuana. But for you this is not even a story. It is an actual thing that happened in an actual place, ergo it was real.

You should point out that you didn't know Claudine L. before this happened. Claudine L. was a Spanish Major from the Sorbonne who lived upstairs from you in a student residence in the Jewish Quarter, not far from the Plaza de Miserere. She was born in Avignon but this fact was learned at an ice-breaking party hosted by the building's concierge and does not represent the establishment of early intimacy. Whenever you think of Claudine L. today you imagine Picasso's *demoiselles*; you imagine her savage and angular with a glowing nakedness that your own body could never achieve. You imagine her skin like oil. It is not a coincidence that her face always seems to be masked. You are thinking of her now and you are outraged by what love can do. You are thinking of Claudine L. bathed in the green light, and how even though you were scared you were also thrilled, because the threat of potential global extinction brought you as close as it was possible to be to the only thing in the world you could not live without. All the time people claim to be unable to live without a great love, or cigarettes. But it is different for you. Claudine L. is somehow, inexplicably, wired directly into you, into your heart. Or maybe your liver. The Romans prized the liver above the heart. If your liver was examined right this minute the omens would all point to one thing, that you could not live without Claudine L. and you would laugh out loud with relief that even the organic matter of your body understood this.

You realise you have not yet mentioned the green light

and this might make things confusing. It might seem that you are trying to talk about Claudine L. when this story is really all about the green light. You are almost ready to talk about it, but you have to build up to these things. Memory sets its own pace. This is what you tell people now you are a qualified therapist. The only way to tell this story is to go back inside it. This is called Playback, a legitimate dramatic technique used to enhance individual spiritual development. Give me your pain, you tell your patients; I will turn it into theatre. Yes, really. You recognise that some people will be sceptical; you may have to give some sort of practical demonstration to prove how this works. It's a myth that you have to use a watch on a swinging chain to relax people into confession. You just need to say the right things. You need to find key words; literally, words that are keys.

For example, to cure loneliness, you might have to take a person back to the place where they were most alone and show it to them, like a mirror, through improvisation. Give it a go, right here, right now. Where was the place you were most lonely? For argument's sake say it was Buenos Aires, city of fair winds. This might be represented with a dance, with scarves to act as the wind. Now you'd describe the specific environment. It's a studio with a balcony, although that is just a way of disguising that you have to eat, sleep and shit in the same room. This you might reflect through miming the closed body, arms hugging your shoulders, restricted, contained. *O that this too too solid flesh would melt*! You have always found Shakespeare an effective tool in your therapy classes, but whether or not you make use of the Bard is wholly dependent on your patient's intellectual capacities.

Move on. Go inside the studio, not in reality, in your mind. Open the door. What can you see? Do you smell anything? This is a really important question because so much of our memory is based on scent. You smell stale fried food and something sweet, like hashish smoke. You smell the cold night air. You smell the strangeness of Tipa trees, old rain, the ancient must of cholera ridden streets, the southern hemisphere. You go into the bathroom and turn the tap just to see if it is true that the water swirls backwards down the plug hole. It is not.

It is from this room that you saw the green light, first bright and then almost immediately exhausted by its own act of shining. Light like an arrow. Not an earthly light, an aquatic glimmer from across the galaxy, reaching into your room as if to say, *we are here*. You instinctively felt that the light was plural, and sentient. Not a dream, just light. Not just light—communication. You want to add that there was no music accompanying the light, no interstellar chimes. That would be ridiculous.

Wait! You see what's happened here. The way you switched roles. If this were an actual patient you could be in real trouble. But the essential principles are demonstrated well enough. Through art you transform the past. From the new past you alter the present. You imagine your father shaking his head saying, 'What the hell was wrong with popping a Prozac?'

Fuck him. You are beginning to realise that this story involves Claudine L. in some elemental way that you could never have anticipated, like when scientists say that life on Earth as we know it wouldn't exist were it not for a series of catastrophes, although you are not sure who is the catastrophe, you or Claudine L. Loving her is what it means to be damaged. If you were to look up *damage* right now, in a thesaurus, there she would be. Probably not smiling, she didn't smile much. You haven't mentioned the mole on her cheek. That incredibly complex braid in her hair that your mother would call a French plait, but to Claudine L. would be just a plait, the same way as in Mumbai no-one calls up for an Indian takeaway.

You only had one conversation with Claudine L. before you saw the green light. You might have said something simple like 'Hey!' or it might have been that a look, one look, replaced all the words you were trembling to say, but immediately you knew you had made a poor impression because one of the laws underpinning civilised society is that a book is almost always judged by its cover.

'Don't you speak any Spanish?' Claudine said. 'That's kind of the point of being here, no?'

'Would English be okay? I'm just more comfortable with English.'

'Of course you are. You can take the British out of the Empire but you can't take the Empire out of the British.'

'I'm sorry, what?'

'What? I didn't say anything.'

Technically you are not British because your father is from Salmon, Idaho, but this is a moot point that you sensed would impress Claudine L. less than allowing her to believe you the embodiment of imperialist evil. Needless to say you were now regretting the fact that for various reasons largely centring around the presidency of George Bush you did not opt to take US citizenship on your eighteenth birthday. Come back! you wanted to shout as she left the building. Claudine! *Por favor*. But she did not turn round. It was the coldest July for thirty years and she went out into the hard, bright air, blowing on her tiny hands, stamping those feet that you wanted to feel pressed against the small of your back in the night. There was even talk of snow that July. You wanted to give her something warm: your hat, your heart. But because you could not, you just waved after her, as if it was all part of the ritual of opening mail.

When you think about it now, it does seem strange that Claudine L. should have chosen to confide in you above everyone else who might have seen the light. You have never heard it said that way before, i.e. aloud. Seen the light. You wonder if it is a signifier for something bigger, something to contradict everything that is known about creation. Even now you think that humanity might be too quick to cling only to things that can be proved. You have always found the significance of opposable thumbs to be faintly alarming, in the same way you never quite came to terms with the truth about Father Christmas.

And you cannot deny semantics. You saw the light. You were standing at the studio window and outside there was the sky, like mercury, or a dangerous dream. There is nothing more unfamiliar than the sky on the other side of the world, and the loneliness made you want to sing just to hear the voice of a human being. From this dark sea came the light, raining down into your room with no warning. It would not be a cliché to describe it in the same terms as water. It was not one light but many lights, concentrated into a single point that hovered on the wall above your head, and what you felt was a terrible, prehistoric kind of fear that extended from a time when if you didn't move fast enough you'd be eaten.

The light moved slowly, as if scanning the room and you wondered if this was happening all across the world. You would at least try to make a case for the human race. On Earth we have all these amazing things, you would say. Telephones the size of a credit card. Biros. But nothing happened. The light changed its mind, withdrew, vanished. You remember now how the rhythm of your heart changed in the fraction of a second before the darkness returned, as if your heart was outside your body, in your hand, and you were watching it beat. You wanted to phone somebody, your mother. You wanted to hear the words, I love you. Or, Sweetie, everything's fine. We're just going shopping. Take care, honey.

In the morning there was a letter in your mailbox for Claudine L. This would have been an amazing coincidence if you had not run into the concierge the night before and offered to help him catch up on the backlog caused by the weather. You waited for her by the front door of your building, assuming a casual position that suggested you had the luxury of choosing whether you would ever go out into the cold; only when you saw Claudine L. in the hall would you look up and move. But it is hard to hold a nonchalant position for more than twenty minutes. More than that, it is hard to be nonchalant when you have witnessed what could well be the Beginning of the End. English or Spanish, every available word you knew seemed ridiculous in the wake of the green light. 'Hey, Claudine, I think this is yours,' was as nonsensical as a limerick.

And yet. As she descended the stairs and you held out the letter you knew straight away this was exactly the right thing to have done. Not one right thing, but the last move in a chain of right things. Sometimes we are faced with decisions that rely on an ancient intuition, as if that moment of extending your hand towards Claudine L. was the culmination of twenty three years of making that same gesture, as if the very first time you stretched your arms in the womb was in preparation for this. She looked right into your eyes. Her look said: she had never seen you before. No. Weren't you–? The one Claudine L. insulted a few days ago. Or maybe you were just The One. This was what you willed her to think. But you had to remain quiet. It was like when you have cheated on a quiz and have to be very careful not to shout out the answers before the question has been asked. If you spoke first, it would be the end. So you waited it out. As soon as she said 'This is a weird question,' you knew it was only a matter of time. When you heard the words 'green light', it was like winning the lottery.

'Do you want to go up to my room and talk, Claudine?'

'Talk? What about?'

'I think it would help. I was really scared. Were you scared?'

'Are you kidding? I was fucking horror-struck. Horror-struck? Is that the right way to say it?'

'It's the best way to say it, Claudine. So do you want to see my room?'

When you were seven, you saw another light. It was Christmas Eve, and it was also the year your best friend's cousin fell out of a window and died, when you had the traditional fascination with death of all seven-year-olds. At seven, death is no more than a secret form of life. The potential annihilation of humanity was therefore not something that particularly alarmed you, although you remember a certain mild anger that it all might disrupt the filling of stockings.

You lived in a much bigger house then, with fields beyond the garden fence. Your father's indiscretions on the living room sofa and your new, exclusive life with your mother were yet to come. As you were looking out of your bedroom window, scanning for reindeer, you saw the light way out in the field, colourless, blinking. You remember a thrilling breeze at your neck. Strange thoughts came to you like bright stars, obvious and old, as if not only had these thoughts been waiting too long to be inhabited but you were the single person they were destined to find. This would be how it would happen. First the lights, then shadows with enormous heads. Tractor beams pushing through gunmetal clouds. A subtle manoeuvre while everyone opened their presents around the world.

Your father told you later that it was just a workman's lamp. The fields were being prepared to make way for a housing estate and the lamp must have been kicked over and forgotten while the site was closed for the holidays. It remained in the garage, still flashing, until your mother cleared the place after the divorce. But this version of events never entirely satisfied you because there are some things about that night you still cannot explain. The urgency of your father's movements as he went out into the snow. Your mother's voice saying, 'See what it is, Brian, for God's sake!'

You don't really know if it happened the way you are telling it now but you have a feeling there are things even seven-year-olds instinctively know to be true. For a long time afterwards this was the picture you carried of your father: a lone figure striding out across the field with a bat swinging against his leg, the snow alight and dim in alternate beats.

Once she was in your room you could detect a lack of satisfaction in Claudine L. too. She touched plates and books like a blind person, trying to feel who you were. But this was just a room in which until the night before, nothing amazing had ever happened and there was not much to feel. She paused at the photograph pinned above your desk. 'You like Humphrey Bogart?'

'That's my father!'

'Shut up! Well, here's looking at you kid.'

'What? Oh, right.'

'Hey, you did see it, didn't you?'

'I guess if you squint…'

'No, asshole, the light.'

You were not used to being called an asshole, but you put it down to Claudine L. being French and didn't hold a grudge, which showed just how much she was doing to realign your core beliefs. When she asked if she could stay with you tonight there was only one answer and it had been waiting light years to be said aloud.

Together you and Claudine L. considered the options. Neither of you knew if the Aurora Australis was visible from the city, and the light was too low for a plane. Claudine suggested terrorists, but these are the things you ask at the time. Later you realised the light was not actually airborne.

It was a grounded light, you guessed maybe two blocks away. That left the one thought neither of you could say aloud, and it was two blocks away. It was knowledge that if spoken had the power to become truth, like when you told your mother about your father and the Polish cleaner. It's obvious now your mother knew about that all along but it was okay, because if a tree falls in a forest and nobody is there to hear it, everyone knows it doesn't make a sound. Then along you came with the trumpets. You had no intention of making the same mistake twice. So instead you said, 'I once knew someone who fell out of a window.'

'Oh.'

'He died.'

'Shit.'

'I'm just telling you because these windows don't look safe. You should sit over here, on the bed.'

Claudine rolled her eyes. 'Are you high? I could use something right now, if you had something.'

You had something. But Claudine didn't have any money, so she offered to make you dinner instead. Her world famous salad.

It was only potatoes and sweet corn, but it was good. Something about the prefix *world-famous* made you see it differently. Superlative potatoes. Never had there been such a creamy mayonnaise. 'It's a secret recipe,' Claudine L. said. 'My grandmother's. I could tell you, but…'

'…then you'd have to kill me.'

She stabbed gently at your arm with her fork and your chest moved like there were wings beating under your ribs. 'I heard some guys talking this morning. That Italian kid with the fucking hideous death metal jacket? He saw it. But I thought I was going mad, until you.'

So that was how it went. She was too afraid to be alone and you had wanted this since you arrived in Buenos Aires. Or maybe not exactly this, but the first rule of life is that you take what you can get. You were like a bodyguard, without the guns, but you didn't mind, because the bodyguard always gets the girl as long as they wait long enough and don't make any sudden moves. You slept together in the same bed, but there was only one bed. You shared vivid intimacies, but the studio really was just one room and it's hard to use a toilet quietly in the night. She was gone every morning to her class in San Telmo and every hour until the evening was unique only because of its varied proximity to her return. In the morning there was no reason to eat or even get out of bed; dinner time and it was like you had been given permission to breathe. The vibrations of the air as she walked about your room, the smell of potatoes boiling, these things became Buenos Aires, which had never looked less like Paris, or even Buenos Aires. You actually hardly knew what the city looked like. You hadn't been to class in two weeks. You knew every inch of your shitty little room, every cockroach out in the hall, but you had not seen a Milonga or wept at Eva Peron's grave. It didn't matter. For years to come you will be able to recall Buenos Aires with a clarity that goes infinitely beyond geographical precision.

You once knew a girl who told you that she fell in love with people, not men, not women. You didn't know what this really entailed, this wild, undefined model of attraction, but when she asked you to go to after-work drinks with her, you said yes, just in case. That night you had too much tequila and would have kissed her if one of your older colleagues hadn't come along to warn you off. This warning travelled with you through the intervening years, alerting you not just to the dangers of the girl who fell in love with people but the whole world, every possible scenario where love might exist. But love did not exist that way here. Whatever it was that Claudine L. felt for you, it depended entirely on the light, and fear, and not knowing. It was almost the exact opposite of a relationship, where the goal was to remove fear and attain a state of complete understanding. Each night you willed the light to return, because the light was the new kind of love. It was more extraordinary even than love. But it didn't come back and there are only so many ways to make mysteries out of ordinary things.

'We should call each other by secret names,' you said, after Claudine L. had been staying with you two weeks. 'I'll be Silver. What about you?'

'Elisabetta. No. I'm not sure about this.'

'Elisabetta?'

'My Mamie's name.'

All the talk of secrets made you feel a little crazy, so when Claudine L. straightened the blanket on the bed you told her your own grandmother had crocheted it while imprisoned by the Nazis. Claudine L. said her grandmother Elisabetta had been in the camps too and maybe that was why you two seemed to have a connection. She said 'the camps' in such a way that you knew she meant one particular camp, but there are some things you can't retract, no matter how hideous.

And it connected you! To this day Claudine L. must think of your grandmother defying Hitler with her yarn and needles. But there is no way back from that kind of lie; distraction is the best you could hope for. So you asked, 'Is that the grandmother who makes the amazing salad?' and she told you no, no that was the other one, this grandmother was shot on the Death March through Poland; the recipe was from her mother's side, the side that didn't know such suffering.

And it could have gone on that way, forever, but in every romance, even the unromantic ones, there is a test, and yours came after three weeks, via Claudine L.'s laptop and the BBC World Service. You learned that plane tagging was a big problem in the cities. Kids were shining hand-held lasers into the cockpits of landing aircraft. An arrest had been made in California, but it was not just America. It was everywhere. It was England, it was Buenos Aires. The point was: the lasers were green. The light was *kids.* It was okay. It was not. Not the thing you were both afraid it would be. But the relief was Claudine L.'s only. She could still stay with you, you wouldn't stop her. But she no longer needed a bodyguard. She didn't need your room or its unacceptably intimate sanitary arrangements. 'I guess I can go home now' hurt as much as a lance in the side.

Claudine L. hunted through the studio, removed eyelash curlers, twenty Gitanes, a box of tampons. You were going to help but instead you grabbed her by the shoulder. 'Stay', you said, and her dress became static, like the fabric was part of your skin, moving in time with your blood. For as long as she stood there, you might still live.

'What?'

'Stay, Elisabetta.'

'There's no need. You heard what they said. Lasers can't hurt you, right?'

'Maybe the lasers are not what *we* saw,' you said. But in this sentence you gave something away, something essential, perhaps in the sadness of the words *we*, or *maybe*, or *lasers*, or *not*. Or in the way you did not say: *I will die if you leave now*.

'They could be wrong about the lasers, Elisabetta.'

'Stop it. They're not wrong. And it's Claudine. That name thing *was* dumb.'

They weren't wrong. And the name thing was dumb. The speed of her departure made you feel dark and mad, like Hamlet, and not for the first time. There are more things in Heaven and Earth, *Claudine*, you wanted to shout behind the slamming door, but really it was just you, alone in a room in which genuinely, nothing amazing had ever happened, and Shakespeare could only ever sound pretentious.

So it ends like this, what happened to you two summers ago, the thing you have chosen to talk about today. It ends with you bumping into Claudine L. in the hallway the morning before the midterm exam you were not ready to take because of this story. She was with the Italian kid in the hideous death metal jacket. 'You remember Alessandro?' she said. 'We're kind of together now.'

'You're together?'

'We're going travelling. Thailand, maybe.'

'Thailand? I want to say be careful. You know, of disease.'

'That's thoughtful.'

'And don't let anyone carry your luggage.'

'No.'

'I hope you'll be very happy. Together.'

'I hope you'll be happy–'

'It's all right. You can say it. Alone.'

You went upstairs. You opened your door, walked inside. You shut it tight, not the door, your heart. You sat on the seat by the perilous windows, looked into the middle distance, towards the place where the green light had been and whispered, *If you come back, take me.* If this were a film, the tragic music would have a reached a crescendo at that moment. Maybe rain would have lashed at the window and your reflection would have dissolved in the weight of that rain. You don't know why people have such a problem with clichés. Clichés are about the truest things you know. It is as if the world is simultaneously nodding when you hear the words *the rain lashed at the windows*. It says: your loss is enormous. It says: even the weather is crying for you. You would have to be living on Mars not to know this.

Your reflection in the window seemed hostile. If you were honest, heartbreak was a disappointment. What you actually wished for at that moment was for your father to be in the room so you could punch his fucking lights out, an ugly desire accompanied by the same exhilaration as when you look at a petrol gauge blinking red and realise that there is either one mile or fifty miles until the next stop. You could pull over now, but still you will drive. The moral of the thought is: perhaps all hatred is like this, a wager in constant, wild need of being defied. Certainly hate accounts for something like seventy-five per cent of your current patient list, people who wake up in the night with a crazy fever to even the score with a more attractive sister or the man who stole a childhood sweetheart. Or mothers. So often it is mothers. You have always been okay with your mother, but it's by no means true of everyone. The Oedipus thing isn't even the half of it.

There was a postcard from Claudine L. this morning, which was why this story was on your mind. Otherwise today would have been nothing special. Routines don't make things any easier. You stand in the shower and wonder how you can trust the shampoo bottle's claims for the welfare of your hair when the packaging company hasn't even got a basic grasp of the apostrophe.

Claudine's postcard was stamped Tucson, Arizona, with a picture of the Grand Canyon on the front, falling away into the mantle of the Earth under a pale brown sun. It is such a familiar landmark and yet it looks so much like a world you cannot possibly know, that even holding it in your hand felt dangerous. It says something about you that the time when you were happiest was based on an error of perception, but as a Drama and Movement Therapist you can probably work out the significance of this for yourself.

You pick up the postcard again now, touch your fingers to the words like they might burn. Then you put on a song by Paul Simon, the one about African skies. The one where he sings of Tucson, Arizona, and wings to fly through harmony. You dance around, loose and free. It is never a good idea to dance on your own, especially in front of a window. Especially not when you are thinking about the light, that first light on Christmas Eve, and your father, out there in the snow taking on the world. You hear his voice every time you walk into your practice, which is really just a room above a Travel Agent with your name stencilled on the door. 'Clap Trap', he is saying. 'You couldn't have been a doctor. Hell, a lawyer even. We threw good money after bad with you.'

In response to your call

Dear G–,

I'm in Paris. The last time I was in Paris was probably the last time I wrote a letter... I'll apologise straight off for my handwriting; I want to say it's screwed from years of typing, but the truth is I'm just impatient, and ink *hurts*. And yes, I have a passport now, I can go anywhere, which is a thing I haven't been able to say for more than ten years, (did I tell you this story? It ends with the lesson: never destroy your marriage certificate, no matter how much you hate the bastard…) The first thing the Immigration guy said to me was—hey, you can flee now if you want to!—like running away was a thing that I'd won. Did I want to? Is this what I'm doing? It was you told me once, all that stands between the moment of disaster and the collapse of humanity is seven days. Or was it less optimistic—five. I try to imagine you striding out against the apocalypse with a gun and can only suppose you must be right. I think what I'm saying is: aren't we all, always, ready to flee, at some level?

I'm writing this from a Salon de Thé on the Rue de Rivoli. The signature drink here is hot chocolate, strong as coffee, the milk served in white china jugs and little rosettes of chantilly cream on gilt-edged saucers. None of it looks particularly generous at first, but I promise you, five minutes in and you're seeing stars. The queue to get in the place was long; I was an hour just in line on the street, not even inside, face pressed to the window looking at the macarons like they were terracotta kings in the Forbidden Palace. Not everyone would consider patisserie to be worth the ordeal—but there's a signature drink! And the age-old question: milk or chocolate in first? The waitress was definitely telling me something about the correct order but I wasn't going to ask her to speak English, thinking the system would be self-evident. Here's a sign the establishment you're in is way out of your usual league; that your drink has a system and an understanding of it cannot be assumed. It goes where? And—when? (A measure of one's loneliness: that there is no-one to turn to and ask. Or this: learned at a talk at the Polar Institute, right before I left: that there are whole islands in 'existence' literally imagined by explorers, willed into being by the enormity of the emptinesses they were trying to chart...)

There is an American girl at the table opposite. Long-haired and kind of hip. She's with a Frenchman—he's older, of course. Sometimes she looks over from her Chocolat Africain and catches my eye and I think of the last time I was with someone this way, doing that thing where the conversation is mostly about figuring out which parts of yourself you're going to need to conceal. And don't think badly of me that I imagine them in bed later—or, no, afterwards; if *sans l'urgence*, they will lie in separate silences, if he will be cold, if this will confuse her—if everyone feels this. Fifty Euros says he'll be fucking someone else this time next year. And yet. Maybe I should have done this; loved less and more often.

I am trying to tell you–. I'm writing everything down as if I will forget it.

When I came here last the beautiful girl I was travelling with was stopped on the steps of the Montmartre funicular by a stranger who wanted to take her photograph. Her surprised face, turning from the light of a winter-pallid sun, that is the picture of her I carry in my mind, as if I were the camera, the composition my own. I was 19 when I came here last, when I last wrote letters. It seems an impossibility that I was ever that age. And then there will be the time when I will think it an impossibility that I was ever 39. Is this the best I can say, that the past seems like a time when I was almost alive? Just this morning I saw something when I crossed the street at Solférino, a bird in the road, hit by a car and thrashing into the tarmac, its neck and legs broken in opposite directions, like someone had stamped on a clockwork toy. Not death throes, life throes, shaking loose the last of its life.

I wonder if this is what I am doing in Paris. I wonder if I am shaking loose the last of a life.

You called me at 3am. It was a mistake, I know that—for you

it would have been what, evening maybe? I'm not good with the time difference. I don't know whether you're even in New York. It is that time of year when there is no way to find you if you do not want to be found. It would have been a pressure in your pocket, an accidental combination of buttons pressed, or missed, at just the right moments—not a decision, not desire. And if most of me believes in Baudrillard's hypotheses of Chance, there is equally a part that made you an island, willed into being. It is just possible that maybe, on the other side of the world, you were writing, looking out of a window, and some word or song made you stop, put down your pen, (oh, who of us really does this?) and this something made me worthy of your call. I know it isn't true, but because I didn't answer–.

They are warriors—not kings—and they aren't in the Forbidden Palace, are they?

What you asked me to tell you was the story of the human heart. But, G–, my heart is tired. It disappoints me that all I can manage is this, and I don't even know if I should send it.

–.

They dedicated the mass for the soul of Paolo Alonso

Which was not a name that meant anything to me until I read about how on a quiet, sunlit morning in old Goa a man named Arthur De Souza woke up to the sound of his wife's tears and typed these words into his Internet blog. Bianca De Souza was luminous in the early sun and her shadow fell long over the room, rippling over tiles, throwing itself with force against whitewashed walls, and in another room, another world, their son stirred in his bed and without realising it came back from sleep into a world that was changed because Paolo Alonso was dead. I am thinking of it now, resting my hands on my own keyboard and imagining the sounds of their morning. The call to prayer, perhaps. I imagine the quieter, subtler sounds of china bowls, the louche chatter of a mynah. The crash of the sea slams through it all, always, the way I imagine it. I smell sweet Indian bread toasting and I am blown away with envy.

I found out about my great-great grandfather in a similar way, by which I mean-chance. It turned out he was once the captain of a famous clipper ship, his saltwater blood connecting me to a long line of men who knew that words like boom do not have to mean a loud noise and the leeway is not just a margin of error. The leeway is in fact when a ship drifts off course from the direction of the wind. This is what I do now, in my mother's garden. I shut my eyes and hold out my arms and cast off. I float on my back against the dead grass and wonder what the sun is like in Goa, whether the light is cool and white in the mornings as in Europe, or dangerous and vital as in the books I read by Rushdie, Desai, Mistry. In these books rain smokes down the mountains like a dragon and the light is weak as tea. The light pours in the place where Arthur De Souza sits typing at his open window. If you stood beneath it you would hear the sound of words falling from his fingers, feel the way his grief hits the page, letter by letter. He would look up, I think, startled by the sound of a footfall beneath the window, only momentarily disturbed as if by a stray cat, or a sudden memory, before dropping his eyes to the keyboard again.

My mother stands above me on the steps of the back porch, looking at me like I am a stranger, and the look I give her, I could be her child again.

I never told you about this distant grandfather, but then I didn't have the time to tell you about a lot of things. A thing I planned to share with you was the time I was chased by a prostitute who was selling garden gnomes by the side of a motorway somewhere outside Bratislava. It's the sort of truth you can't put in a story because who would believe it? At best it's a good after-dinner anecdote. But we hadn't long moved off the *Cat in the Hat*, so you were not ready for this kind of memory, the kind that alerts you to the existence of that remote time when your mother was not your mother, which is a time not one person on Earth is comfortable hearing of.

Outside the clinic it is turning to spring and a wind blows the light across the glass like a squall coming in from the sea. For a minute, sitting in the milky light, I am invisible; Ramani, in front of me, is invisible. A wildness takes me. My mother, who taught pre-school children, used to say that on a windy day the children become savages, but Ramani isn't familiar with this phenomenon and she doesn't comment. She sucks on the end of her pen and reviews her notes, the ones she made last week. The light stays outside the window for a moment and then rushes in like it's coming for us, and suddenly we are neither of us there, as if we have simply been returned to molecules of Hydrogen and Oxygen. I imagine we are both holding our breath. I think of Ramani as air and I water. And then suddenly I feel too light, as if it is no longer enough to simply speak of water; at this moment, I need to be submerged.

I tell Ramani the end of that other story, the one about the grandfather who jumped overboard in a mutiny and drowned in the Java Sea. Joseph Conrad later wrote about it, which is the only thing I can say about my life that is genuinely interesting. I don't know the end of Paolo Alonso's story. I worry that it was a gun, or terrorism. People use the phrase *in cold blood* when they talk about violent death, but this is not how people die. People die in heat. Even the ones who choose their own death, they die trying very hard to find a reason to want to stay alive.

I tell Ramani about Paolo Alonso and how on the morning of his funeral Arthur De Souza blogged that he would take his young son to Mass, and they would dedicate the mass for the soul of Paolo Alonso. What Ramani does is sit back in her chair and write, very slowly, on a square, unlined notepad: *they dedicated the mass for the soul of Paolo Alonso*. And then she waits for my cue, which I won't provide because it is me paying her and not the other way around, so it is only right that she should have to work to get the answers she wants. I tell her it is a Latin American name and she nods slowly, as if she is trying to remember something. Then she writes something I cannot see.

She asks if I have ever tried writing a blog, if I think this was a way for Arthur De Souza to heal himself of the grief he felt for Paolo Alonso. I tell her that I don't really know that I can understand Arthur De Souza's grief. She asks if that's because grief itself is hard to understand and I tell her no. No, absolutely not. I tell her that ultimately it's easy to understand grief, but what is hard is the *process* of comprehension, like algebra, which is impossible until you let go of the basic neural reluctance to view letters in place of numbers. And once you learn that it is possible to find x simply by knowing a and b, it's possible—it's *possible*—to understand anything. Relativity. The appeal of reality television. The fact that there is no special reason why you, you personally, would be exempt from suffering.

But it's not for this kind of armchair philosophizing that I pay forty bucks an hour.

❧

My geography—it never was very good. Is Goa a part of India? Ramani wants to know if I think that is significant, the fact I am not fully aware of my place in the world—in its histories of grieving. I tell her I don't believe so but then, I have never really thought about it before. I feel as geographically grounded as any of us can, living as we do on a planet that is dependent on the random turn on its axis, that depends in turn on the continued nuclear fission of a dying star. 'Fission,' I ask her. 'Is that the right word?' Ramani writes this all down, shorthand. 'If you're interested,' she says, 'Goa is a province in South West India.'

'It's like Stingo eating a banana while Sophie's daughter is led to the gas chamber,' I say. But then I am suddenly not sure what I mean, or even whether Sophie's choice was her daughter or her son, or if it was about something else entirely.

'That's a fiction,' Ramani says. 'That didn't actually happen.'

Still, I wonder what it was I was doing on the day Paolo Alonso died. If I was here, on Great Eastern Street, answering Ramani's questions, while he was dying, if it was fast, if there was time for him to pass on a message to those he loved.

'You do know it was just a book,' she says again and louder.

I understand. She has to establish if I have any grip on reality whatsoever.

❧

I do not pay the forty dollars up front. When I leave her office I will give Ramani's secretary a manila envelope containing two twenties, because these days the hole in the wall doesn't dispense anything less—to make the slide towards terminal debt even faster, Martin says. Since June of last year cards or cheques are no longer acceptable; high banking charges, the secretary tells me. Martin tells me this is nothing to do with the banks but a way of avoiding tax. 'You don't need some quack to tell you what's wrong with you,' he says. 'You don't need to pay to hear that.'

In this regard, he is right. My mother would be happy to tell me for free. But what can I say? I need the questions. Isn't it obvious, I want to say, don't you see that if Ramani asks me enough questions, one of them is going to throw up an answer. Like the chimpanzee who would type the works of Shakespeare, if you had a lifetime to wait. I am like a chimpanzee with a typewriter, I will try and tell Martin. It has to happen, eventually.

'And if you get an answer,' he says, 'What then?'

A sudden hail splinters through the sun, hitting all the window sills in turn before clotting into deep amber quarters of light, and what I am reminded of is fireworks, or rather, the November Fifth when my father sat us down and told us that my mother hadn't lived up to his expectations and he was going to live in Germany, where a girl with a distant connection to the heir of a luxury car manufacturer would make him happy in ways my mother would later read about in the back pages of a well-known magazine. 'Are you sure you wouldn't prefer to talk with our bereavement counsellor?' Ramani says quietly.

'I'm happy with you,' I say. 'Really.'

I tell her how I imagine Paolo Alonso's Mass to be. Incense and magic. Shadows and light. She says I am confused. Maybe I am thinking of black mass, which is another thing altogether.

'I'm not even a Catholic,' I say.

Ramani's face does not change. I tell her that Martin came round last night to change my light bulb.

She says, 'Remind me. Martin is your neighbour?'

'Martin's my neighbour.'

'Perhaps,' she says, 'changing your own light bulb would give you some sense of independence. I think you need that. I think that would be good for you.'

'I am independent,' I say. 'My independence isn't compromised by Martin.'

But I will wonder. The next time he stops by to wax the runners of the kitchen drawer that sticks, I'll make a concerted effort to watch the motion of his muscles, marvel at the fluctuation of them under his skin. I imagine myself easing the candle against the sides of the drawers, rubbing it gently the way he does until the drawer gives way in a crash of silver, the disaster that would result. I am okay with this, if it is dependence. It is never me who asks him to stay. When he fucks me I feel his skin is strong, and mine is like tissue paper softly wrapping my bones. All I can say of this is that it seems to help.

I tell her again, 'Martin's just my neighbour.' This is

true, in spite of how it sounds. I know nothing else about him, other than that we shop at the same store; we are both insomniacs, looking for ways to kill time before morning.

In Goa they drink Chai, sweet and spicy, but here it's just tea, with sugar, with sympathy. 'Let me fix you a drink,' he said that first time I invited him in, because I was shivering. Fix my heart, I wanted to tell him. Fix my *heart*.

Another time we talk about emotions. For example, if I had to sum up this year in one word–. Just one word, Ramani says gently, as though she is coaxing the word out, asking it to step into the space between us in her room above Great Eastern Street so that we can look at it, and deconstruct it together. Deconstruction is something that Ramani holds in high regard. Only when we have learned to be destructive can we become constructive beings. *Together* is another word she likes to use. Together we will survive this journey. There will be ups and downs, mountains to climb, but we will tackle them together. She talks to me like I am an animal in a rescue centre. In response, I eye her straight, like a dog. 'Anger,' I say. 'I'm angry that you and I ever had to meet.'

'Okay,' she says softly. 'But who are you angry *with?*' She pauses. 'Are you angry with yourself?'

Ramani asks me about the last conversation you and I had. She asks me to recreate it, perhaps even to finish it. This I can do. We have tried the telephone call I would most like to have and the letter I wish I could write, with little success. Strictly speaking it wasn't a conversation, more a question left hanging because I could not answer it; did the Chandlery department of Mulligan's sell candles or sailing equipment? Candles, surely, I thought to myself. Air conditioning raised up our hair. I rushed you, grousing, through women's clothing, then Electricals. We were in Gardening. Then Toys. You were in Toys. First we were marching, then gliding, unencumbered. When I turned, knowing how the lack of effort was wrong, I could see the departments stretching back like a kaleidoscope, but you had gone.

Terry towel shorts, I told the security guard when he asked what you were wearing. With little flowers. But I couldn't remember the exact colour of your t-shirt or whether or not you had taken a hat with you. Later, when the police had finished up their preliminary work in the store I wondered if it would be all right to ask someone—was it boats? was it candles?—so that when you came home I could tell you the answer.

The details are where you find the real anger. A chandler, I will be forever aware, is both a candle maker and a merchant of marine equipment. It is a city in Arizona south-east of Phoenix, a winter resort with a population of 241,000. Chandler is the emotionally stunted one from *Friends*. It is a word that derives from the Vulgar Latin *candelarius*.

'Vulgar Latin?' I ask Ramani. 'Is that, like, Roman porn?'

I am trying to tell Ramani something else, but what I keep saying is the name of Paolo Alonso.

She says, 'But you don't know Paolo Alonso,' and fiddles with her pen, which appears to be inexplicably dry.

'No.'

At least... No. I don't know Paolo Alonso. But I am no longer sure what knowing is. You know things and then the things you knew change, like the cloud I once saw in the shape of Jesus. I knew it was Jesus straight away, because of the beard. But it only took ten minutes to turn from the son of God to a map of southern Europe, minus Sicily. We see what we want to see, is what I want to tell her. It doesn't even matter why.

I tell Ramani how our conversation would go, how it would finish. You would say, I want some sweets, Mama, and I would say, with aching maternal frustration, Ada, do you never stop wanting things?

From underneath the sour smell of the hawthorn at Ramani's open window comes the scent of waiting rain, still vapour. There was a woman, I say—because the silence is worse than the words—there was a woman who saw the face of Marlene Dietrich in a piece of toast.

Her bewilderment frightens me.

My mother saw a ghost when she was five years old. Being five she wasn't afraid; in fact she looked straight into its face and held its gaze. But a ghost doesn't really have a gaze, my mother said, it looks through you and around you, but it doesn't meet your eye. Some evenings I stand in the window for a long time. I wonder if maybe children will go home and tell their parents there is a ghost in the house at the end of the street, the one where the cats got into the bins two weeks ago and there are still roast chicken carcasses under the azaleas.

Against the cold kitchen wall my thoughts ripple darkly, like the sea under a new moon. Things still have to be done, little things like closing the curtains in the spare room when the streetlamps come on. And such strange things; locking the door when I use the bathroom. In case the dog comes in?

There is a lot of space in my apartment. I walk into a room and I feel the space, not the things that are there. Sometimes I have to just lie down and wait, the space feels so heavy. Slowly the objects move in to fill the gaps, like people entering a dark cinema. I smooth down the sheets on the bed. I arrange the toy animals in a line, biggest to smallest. How eager are all the little stuffed faces. I move the rabbit closer to the Disney princess doll, away from the Wile E. Coyote.

I think I feel you behind me, but it is only the dog, again.

After you leave the world, how long is it before it is like you were never there? What frightens me now: how long will it be until it is like *I* was never there?

Yesterday I went to the coast. I took the train, skimming out through maize fields until just by looking at the sky you could tell you were getting closer to the sea. I read *The Story of India* by Michael Wood and ignored the conductor when he asked me to take my feet off the seat beside me. My shoes were clean. They were my favourite sandals, the black ones that are almost impossible to match with anything that seems appropriate for someone who has passed forty. Here is the question: what should I change? My shoes, or my life?

There are little shops on this stretch of coast selling the

kind of expensive shit that appeals to people like me, we who appreciate pretty things and have not much else to do but spend money acquiring them. But here is the problem: there are never enough pretty things to buy to make up for all the world's ugliness. I bought olive bread and organic hummus from an artisan deli because it made me feel a better person than if I'd chosen the supermarket kind, and I ate it on the Palace Pier, with sand blowing into in my mouth and the sound of the Kash Kong brash against the humming sea. The *rentrée* the French call this kind of wind, a wind of beginnings and restorations. How quickly this time is over. How quickly the year becomes something finished. A speckled landscape of rain, no longer yet to be.

The last time I came here, it was summer and the pier was full of tourists and final year students giddy with a sense of being released into a bigger world. The sky was wide and high, white clouds in brave symmetry with the water that swirled beneath ironwork arches. I visited the Psychic in her tent by the Super Booster, because this was before I had discovered Ramani's office in the clinic on Great Eastern Street. 'Don't tell me *how*,' I said, suddenly afraid the tangled woodland she could see might be real after all.

Outside, I watched the Super Booster roar and dive. Suddenly nothing could engage me quite as much as the sight of people voluntarily handing over money to be suspended above the ocean in a tiny cage. Like animals they queued. For ten dollars you got to gaze down on the crowds, see the pier lights from above where they appeared pinpricks only, fragile little constellations that gave the illusion of being close enough to touch. The cage climbed towards the purple blaze of the evening. Then it plunged. There was no way of knowing if the screams were whoops of pleasure or fear as the cages rushed down to meet the pier. But the queues to ride didn't get any smaller and the purr of the sea was constant, like the radio you don't notice until it's switched off. Such a funny hunger, was what I thought. To let go, to fall.

When I said *better*, I meant more successful. When I say successful, I mean: someone who doesn't pay forty bucks an hour for the privilege of recalling the worst things about their lives, I suppose.

Ramani's secretary asks if she can get me a coffee, flicking through the magazines that are meant for us, the clients. The hair style she is looking at won't suit her. For a heart-shaped face you want a chin-length bob, or layers swept around the temples, even if they do block a clear line of vision and cause you to develop the nervous habit of flicking your fringe out of your eyes. I contemplate telling her this and then I think, save yourself the trouble, let her screw things up for herself.

Years ago I was a nurse. I have heard a man told, at his post-operative briefing, 'You are mistaking pain for the sensation of eating.' I wonder if I am mistaking pain for the sensation of living. Is that what Arthur De Souza felt when he sat at his typewriter, plunging down the keys in a frantic bid to feel everything solid, because if he was to feel anything at all it had to hurt? There are people who sit in Ramani's waiting room who rub at their scars lovingly, with longing. It is her job to cure them of the urge, but maybe they are better the way they are. Maybe they are the only ones who still know what it means to feel.

The first moment I held you, wet and pink and squealing, I thought: you will suffer pain because *I* want you here. It is a mathematical certainty.

Inside her office I look past Ramani and there I see Bianca De Souza in her nightgown by the window, the morning sun spilling across old Goa and down over her shoulders so that when Arthur rises from his typewriter he is momentarily struck by the impression that there is an angel at the balcony. I imagine Goa like you remember a dream. The sunlight is not gold but an old light, the colour of centuries. From some angles the world is bleached. The world is under six foot of perfect snow. It is the kind of light that reminds you that once Romans built roads across Europe under the same sun. Once my great-great-grandfather floundered in the Java Sea. Arthur De Souza sits under the Goan sun and looks at his wife in wonder, the way she shimmers just out of sight, there and then not there, like the lenticular images in his son's picture books.

I imagine Bianca to be such a beautiful woman, the kind that Arthur De Souza has been waiting for all his life. Love is not strange; the songs are wrong about that. Love is obvious. I don't suppose Arthur De Souza has ever listened to the Everley Brothers, but what do I know? Almost immediately, something else occurs to me: ask a woman whether, if faced with the choice, she would save her lover or her child and she will say, without hesitation; my child. Ask a man the same question and first he will weigh up the options. A father's love is a different thing. And so Arthur De Souza would throw himself in front of the bullet whose silent trajectory arced towards his wife. And so he would hold her back, screaming, if she made to do the same for her son.

When they leave for Mass he will say a prayer to say thank you for bringing Bianca to him. But he will also ask God the question, why did you then take Paolo Alonso? Why is it that you put sadness in the very marrow of our bones?

I hope he is at peace, I want to say to Ramani—*Paolo Alonso*. But instead I tell her something that I learned only yesterday, about how Portuguese names flood through Goa because of imperialism. Four hundred years ago Paolo Alonso's ancestors came ashore from across the Arabian Sea, making love to beautiful Indian women, heading inland to populate the new settlement of Vasco da Gama. A city named for a discoverer and pillager of worlds.

Somewhere in the world there is no longer Paolo Alonso. But until he had died, I didn't even know he had been alive. Somewhere in old Goa, there is Arthur De Souza, heading to Mass, who will never know that tonight, walking home from Ramani's office, I will go into the United Reformed Church on Trumpington and use all my loose change to burn a tea light in Paolo Alonso's name.

I look out of Ramani's window towards where the rain sheets in from the west, which is where you find the old magic. I put out my hands, actually hold them out in front of me and see they are shaking, not the involuntary tic of a nervous disposition but wild, violent tremors that push dangerous vibrations through my chest. The sound of my heart is a waiting wonder, like a piano un-tuned and wanting. I feel as if I am about to fall.

And then from somewhere dark in my throat I say–.

I say–.

'Okay, that's good now,' Ramani says, because perhaps this is the start.

All the things

Offer

The time my heart froze over, I was not exactly surprised. It seemed as inevitable as cancer, especially considering I hadn't heeded any of the standard warnings; I had not even bothered to protect myself with a layer of bravado, or lie on social media, which was what all the kids were doing. The man I had left was older, smarter, he liked his girls to be pretty, or nubile, and I was neither, though perhaps if I'd actually tried. At night I heard the disappointment in his voice like a bird-call at my throat. It didn't help that in this man's presence my own voice was non-existent, a frostbitten breath where once there had been words.

When I gave the doctor my symptoms—a scratching inside my chest, a polar chill in rooms I had entered—it was hard to gauge her level of concern. Was this a thing that happened all the time? There were options, if I was unafraid of less conventional routes towards recovery. Therapy was fashionable, but scepticism was co-morbid of my condition, I learned. You do what is recommended though. You do what another person considers the appropriate thing for a life they have never inhabited.

The doctor touched the hexagonal blooms of frost across my chest—*breathe in*!—and prescribed two things, heat and fire, writing it out on a notecard for me to take to the pharmacy. I wanted to ask her about doses, about how you'd know when you'd had too much. Could there be side effects? I wondered, anxious to get things right. 'What's too much?' the doctor said, signing the card with a flourish of blue ink. 'You don't need to worry about *too much* until you've had *enough*.'

Acceptance

From the beginning there was administration; it was all about targets, success was only ever measured by quantitative means. I had no opinion of this. My heart is a block of ice, I felt like reminding the doctor's assistant, who was in charge of the paperwork. It's not like I have a gallstone.

'What's a problem for you?' the assistant asked, matching her sympathy to a graph on the wall: an impression of care was considered an appropriate level given that my condition was in some camps seen as self-inflicted. I repeated my diagnosis, knowing this didn't even begin to cover it, curious to hear what it sounded like when said aloud. I wanted to find some kind of explanation. I tried this: 'I fix people,' I told her. 'I show them what's wrong and I help them find what they're looking for.' What I did not tell her was the thing they were looking for was never me. I did not tell her that I was never the person who was fixed. When you know this is how it works, you put certain measures in place. You get pragmatic. You get cold. You see everything as a kind of contract. I wanted to tell the doctor's assistant: pragmatism is the real problem for me.

The assistant said before the doctor could assign the appropriate treatment I had to pick a verb, one verb to live by for a year. It was not a trick question, not a test. It was a symbol of *doing* something; unusual, but the first step was about trust, or belief in things whose outcomes you couldn't see. 'Two things I don't have,' I joked. But it wasn't a joke. When I realised I was living with this as fact, I wanted to get my coat. I wondered if I could live for a year with anything, whether something existed that wouldn't damage me if I had to spend every day with it, shaping my thoughts, pushing me in one direction or other. It seemed to be such an arbitrary thing, the possibility of living by a singularity of any kind.

The assistant searched the contents of a tulipwood box on her desk. 'Emerge,' she said finally, unfolding the tight square of construction paper. We looked surprised. Our mutual confusion gave us reason to think, for a minute, we might be the kind of people who could enjoy a glass of wine together, if I could... if she wasn't... *Emerge?*

'I'll try,' I told her, but we neither of us knew if I was lying, if this was part of the condition or if it was something I could keep in front of me like a map. Later I realised: the word made no demands. It was me who was asking something of it, wanting it to have the power of a spell. 'Is the treatment going to hurt?' was all I really wanted to know. The language did not exist for how much I wanted to know that.

By way of reply the doctor's assistant gave me an advice leaflet, which I understood would answer those kinds of questions with the professional semantics of promising one thing while meaning everything else. I just wanted an approximation. A rough end of a scale. You could have brain surgery while awake and singing. If it would stop the thing that was stopping you, you would do it, I reasoned, you would take the pain, you would screw up your eyes and cry while they fixed you, even if it felt more like dying than living. The most likely point for significant discomfort was right at the beginning, the leaflet explained, before you had learned to normalise things. But this was a small price. It would be like laser eye correction. It would be like unlocking a dam and letting the bones of a desiccated valley flush with green.

I read magazines in the foyer until the assistant returned. 'Your treatment plan,' she said, which meant more than just a way to get well. 'And if I could draw your attention to the small print...'

Who reads the small print? When I stepped outside onto the street I could hear singing, because it was the summer we were all suddenly experts on football and the sky was white, the sun was veiled, suddenly we were seeing the far-away world up close, or as if from the other side of something, in translation.

Intention

The dream analyst was young, still absorbed in the labyrinths of his own night terrors; I couldn't say my doubts didn't show. I came straight from the office, distracted by the joke

Luiz told me as I was leaving. 'He's flirting,' my friend said.

'Who is?'

'You really don't know anything, do you?'

Here is what I know, I thought. It is impossible to explain loneliness to anyone when by definition, if someone starts to listen, you're doing better than you were ten minutes ago. But this doesn't mean the loneliness goes away. It is the opposite of seeing something that isn't there. It is seeing nothing when there is a whole island in front of you that somehow all the world's cartographers missed.

I nearly missed my stop because after years the council finally cut back the yew trees by the cemetery and I didn't recognise the street when viewed without distortion, as if every time I had passed through here before today I had been blindfolded, or as if I had never even known sight. I wondered if this had anything to do with the fact that for a long time I was wearing my hair short. I turned to the seat next to me. There was no-one there with whom to share my reasoning, to debate the validity of the article I read about the links between hair and sensory perception discovered during the Vietnam War.

People do this thing in a therapy session, any kind of therapy, trying to make out they don't understand why they are there. I looked confidently at the Dream Analyst, certain he would see past the evidence in my file if I talked fast. But still I couldn't disguise it, my glacial murmur loud in the stone-smooth basin of his room. A pervasive and mid-level iciness was what the analyst detected, difficult to treat in as much as it required a trigger to begin the process; a flood could be expected but you had to wait, for spring, for the end of the world. 'Bring it on,' I said, long fascinated by apocalypse.

My dreams were mostly textbook; teeth, naked attendance at conferences—there was one about a big cat, a lion I thought, stalking the rooms of an unfamiliar apartment, that made the dream analyst consult a colleague. 'Are you sure there's nothing else?' he asked, exasperated. 'Something we can work with?'

The fourth time I visited there was a new and unexpected thing. I told him how… I told him, at night I imagined myself a lover, the fire of the southern hemisphere scalding my cold and silvered skin. A weight low in my belly, something in other circumstances you might call pain but here I understood to be...to be… Okay, this is what I imagined, I told the analyst. The bridge of limbs; one, wild current between them. The force of the sea. The light, and the deep water. The low ocean moan. I meant to say the word *sonorous* but what came out was something different, something that made the analyst sit straight, as if now he was listening, now he was involved. 'That's better,' he said, catching his breath, adjusting his tie.

The scale measured me at *ablative*, surging with something but resisting thaw, which made it sound as though even my unconscious wasn't trying to help. 'Why the southern hemisphere?' the dream analyst wanted to know. 'The body remembers,' I started to say, but I couldn't think what it was remembering, given that all I had done that day was stand talking to Luiz at the Xerox machine. I had the urge to fall back inside my sleeping self, suddenly seeking the dream analyst's permission to speak of the things it could see.

More than once I caught the analyst staring at his lap, as if there the answers were hidden. He seemed to think it was significant, the fact I was distancing my dream-self to the other side of the world, to a place I had never been. 'But what is *this*?' I kept asking him, meaning the wild, agitated blur in my chest that was starting to come at inopportune times. I had no words; it felt a little like the stomach ache you get before an exam, a little like the thing that divers get, the intoxication that comes from being in a world that is doing everything it can to get you to leave.

'Progress,' the dream analyst replied, but he looked doubtful, knowing all the things I didn't.

Consideration

There seemed no logical reason why I could think only of mountains. Or not mountains but the air moving through certain valleys like gun smoke, the way it did nowhere else in the world. Luiz showed me photographs of skyscrapers and watermarked skies. Even though these things were not mine, I missed them like a world I had left without meaning to. I noticed the spaces where he had been, not understanding it, the way I had a sudden eye for absence, the way presence now felt like something large inside a very small space. Something as simple as a staircase could now be measured in terms of *he was there*, or *he was not*.

I asked the light therapist if she had something... I searched a moment for the word. I thought the word was *pelagic* but I didn't want to give anything away. She could offer St. Ives, or St Tropez, there were other beatified towns.

Mostly what was in the bottles was azure, turquoise, hard-and-bright; I avoided those marked 'sparkling'. I was intrigued by one labelled 'Finistere; rough, wet', but this was reserved. Giverny I could send away for—marbled and lenticular, still and moving, both—but the wait was long. The Impressionists liked that one, the therapist reminded me, showing me pictures of gold-dusted fields, the light rich and fatted with flowers. Evening light was the hardest to come by. The catalogue presented a pale violet kind, pierced by the Southern Cross, but this was out of stock with no expected date of return. With the suddenness of sunset, I felt lost, remembering Luiz's hands on my shoulders. Then my mouth at his, my back at the office door, surprised we had found our way there so soon and with such certainty.

You were supposed to use the light sparingly, that was the first thing to understand. The therapist seemed bewildered, or perhaps unused to such particular requirements. She concentrated on getting the right proportions, one eye closed to aid the immersion in her craft. 'But,' I asked her, suddenly unsure of the consequences, 'what happens if this *works*?'

My icebound heart blew a sudden blackness, a familiar chill that I welcomed like a night breeze. Everything I knew was about living with it, not living without. I waited to hear what the light therapist advised. You sink or swim, she said, setting down the bottle, which was the shape of something you'd imagine buying from an old perfumery in Cairo if you were the kind of person who liked to imagine things in terms of their comparison with places and times where they didn't belong. I hesitated. It wasn't a recommended blend, or as popular as the romantic, desert island kind—but there was something. I touched my forehead to the glass, breathed in cypress and the dust of the Highlands. I didn't know if the light therapist had given me all this or if I was already part of it, if I was being changed, atomically. 'You wanted heat and fire?' she said.

I drank it down, bathed in it, rolled and swallowed and twisted and sang. The light poured down from the bottle neck and took with it everything it touched, the stopper, the label, my dress, my fear. I wanted to plummet, I wanted to dive. I sucked at the last drops. My legs opened and twitched, remembering fins.

Later, sticky and light-drunk, exhausted by shining, I found the label curling at the foot of my slipper: River of January, looking two ways.

Terms

For two hundred pounds the flyer promised we would learn the one word that was required to achieve our heart's desire. Seduced by language, we filed into a hall crescent-mooned with plastic chairs, our breath damp, our cardio-vascular systems giddy with anticipation.

To begin with, as a group, we couldn't decide: did our hearts desire love, or success or… the something else, the wordless thing, was heavy and unspoken across the room. There was an uneven split between love and whatever the things were that money could buy. We were not sure whether happiness counted as anything, or whether that was a by-product, not something we could aim for straight off, if we even had a right to ask for it anyway.

It was an old hall and we felt the facilities did not match the price of our ticket. While the convenor was fixing the projector I asked the woman next to me what she had come here to find. 'All the things,' she said, like it was obvious. 'I tried everything else. Past life regression. Those little blue tablets that look like M&Ms.' Her tone was hushed. 'Dildos. Did you try that?' I hadn't. I thought of the joke about the man who didn't care how he was reincarnated as long as he had a huge cock, which made me think about what it is like to sleep with a person, really sleep with them, the pressure of their foot against your foot or the fact that sometimes you are knitted together and other times it's like you have forgotten who the other is, only to turn, startled—*you, yes*!—and I felt a brief, rushing, fluid surge before it hardened inside me again, before wisps of condensation iced my breath, which made the woman next to me raise her eyebrows as if to say, yes, this is what it's like, *all the time*. A quiet girl in the back row looked away, afraid of what we could do.

How would we know when we had found what we most desired? Would it be obvious, unequivocal, like matching the numbers on the lottery? The convenor seemed exhausted by the questions. It was like, he said, nobody had read the posters. It was as if none of us were serious about wanting to know. A number of us, a separatist group, seemed to doubt the requirement for just one word. It stood to reason that we were the talkers; more than one of us worked in academia. An hour in we revealed other, unexpected difficulties, including the fact that most of the women in the room were also the kind of people who assumed every man to be a potential axe murderer. We challenged the convenor; what we desired was complicated, a constant vacillation between desire itself and the fear of death. The quiet girl at the back spoke up for the first time. 'You think it's that,' she said. 'But what you're really caught between is death and the fear of desire.'

We sat in silence for a few minutes, thinking about this. I say *we*; how was I know to know what the group was thinking? In the dark quiet of the hall I remembered how Luiz told me to walk away as soon as I thought I wanted to stay. I let myself hold that thought for a moment longer than I needed. I braved it out. I have a word, I told the convenor. I picked up my bag. I didn't speak it. I held the word in my mouth instead. *Um beijo*, two feelings at once, of being cast away, and longing; a feeling of being shipwrecked and also of sighting land.

Performance

Luiz told me the story of a man who came home to find his wife fucking the neighbour on the couch. How what the man thought was: well, I can sell the couch. I wanted to explain that here we are not so different in our denial. It would just be that we were less entrepreneurial. All the couches of the world could be moving in the room behind us but still we would wait the four minutes that is the proper requirement to steep a perfect cup of English Breakfast tea before springing to action.

The homeopath explained the final stage of rehabilitation.

There would be a series of shots, each one building a tolerance based on the idea of triggering the natural system of healing, treating like with like, a small dose to ward off something bigger, influenza, or some unnamed lovesick fever. I gave her my arm. It was an insurance policy. What my head might forget, every cell in my body would become programmed to fight.

I wanted it to be my legs that swung to the floor as the couch was sold from under me. When I told the homeopath this she looked interested. She asked me what it was I was looking for. Someone who eats, I told her. Someone who shouts my name when he comes. The ice slipped into me, drop after drop. I held my breath. Nothing changed. My blood continued to move, tepid, following an ancient rhythm it recognised, understood. 'Does that feel ok?' she asked, slowing the flow.

'Yes,' I breathed. 'Yes. Yes. And, *yes*.'

The homeopath suggested we could be cautiously optimistic. Still, relapse was the big worry. 'You're afraid of something, you embrace it,' she said. 'You pick up a tarantula. You climb the biggest goddamn tower you can find.' I understood what she was saying. The only way to tell if the treatment had worked was to overdose.

That night I went out. I touched everything I could, pulled it close, breathed it in. I walked into bars, called out men's names, gave them my coat without waiting to be asked. I left change in the hats of homeless people. I stared in the windows of expensive shops and let kim chi run down my chin. Still the warmth rose, still nothing stopped it. I felt it building, the pressure, the furious wave in my cunt, and it was hard to know what to do with it, too much of everything; I wouldn't say the one word it was not allowed to become.

I returned to the treatment plan, devoured the advice leaflet. There was a small chance, it said, of basal slippage, a sudden internal, fluid movement that would accelerate the longer term shift towards warming—disconcerting in the immediate, but ultimately, safe: ultimately, a step in a permanent right direction. It was the very opposite of everything on which the future of humanity depended. It was the disaster all the scientists of the world were trying to prevent. I couldn't think why I hadn't noticed this before. Such a basic question not to have asked: what was worse—the memory, or the unknown? It seemed unfair to expect words to describe how that felt any more than asking what we see of a star to tell us how fast it burned.

I knocked on Luiz's door. I climbed the stairs, got into bed, let it flood out of me; the run-off, tears, salt, the sea. All the things I had no use for. Who cared if I cried. Who cared if we drowned. I let myself break the dark pools of his eyes, allowing the cliché because what the hell. I swam in him, pulled him down and up and in until there was nowhere left to go but inside each other's scars; there was a fierce pulse at all the places he had been. *Oh*, I wanted to shout to the shuddering air. Oh. *Oh*. When Luiz slept, I kicked off the blankets, restless with the heat of another person's skin. Maybe it was that or maybe it was the heat of my own skin. I didn't have to decide. I thought of the writer who said that sometimes one meets a woman who is beast turning human, and felt a savage ache along my soaking wet thighs. I touched his hand. He did not touch mine back.

This is why you read the small print, I thought, although even if you did... Even then.

Uncertainty

I visited the doctor in the morning, thinking: *enough*. Without the heavy wall of ice in my chest, I had no ability to process comparisons. Enough is just a word in the same way the sum of the three angles in a triangle will always equal 180°. Little things were lodging in the places that had once been glassed over; a preference for old cartoons, certain sandwiches. I thought of the woman who was looking for all the things and realised; there was no middle ground. You wanted it all or you didn't.

Was there a counterweight? Was there some kind of retainer that a person could fit—*there*—holding in place what was just right, no more, no less. I knew the answer already, before I even sat down. This was the risk you took. This was the palm tree, swaying tall in a formerly barren plain. You wouldn't wish it away if it meant returning to tundra. But you wondered if you could live with it, that feeling of life in you, photosynthesis or whatever scientists wanted to call it, could you live with it if there was no-one to—

—no-one to—

You tell yourself you can, because that is the only way.

'Tell *me*,' the doctor said. 'Anything you want to say.'

I said his name. I said it like a promise, like a person trying to find faith. I heard the word, at first thrilling and then it was clear that all along it had been nothing more than a sound.

If you were going to suspend the treatment, there were things you had to understand. It wouldn't be like it had never happened, the doctor explained. It would be like, like–.

A burn, which changed the layers you couldn't see even after the blistering had settled and the new skin grew. At a place you couldn't measure, or even touch, the change would be irreparable, but you could bear it, that was the assumption, the statistics were good, at least in those who had kept up the programme in other ways. Was that what I wanted?

Was it what I wanted? It was now or never. It was sink or swim. I was sitting on the cot, my feet under me like a child about to listen to a story. I felt a mild panic, unsure for a minute if I had ever wanted to be cured. Hook me up, I told the doctor. *Now.* I watched the lines of my heart gather on the monitoring screen, bunch together, separate, press again together, together, together. The movement where there had been nothing, not even paralysis. My body called. My heart had responded. Are you sure? the doctor was saying. Are you *sure?*

How can I tell you? It was like this, like when you are in control of something, a food blender, a car, and you have to learn to balance the pressures of too much and not enough. I pressed down. I felt the roar, pulled it back, waited to find the bite. I could go under. I could raise my hand, cut it down through the water, pull it back, stroke forward.

'Swim,' I whispered, fiercely, feeling the fire, willing it to keep burning.

It wasn't Stockhausen's

The ward is lit like the sky before a thunderstorm and from his bed Bill Hare can see right to the end, but only in the one direction, towards the nurses' station. The other side is as unknown to him as the dark side of the moon. He tells his consultant oncologist this as a joke, and two days later she puts a book on his bedside locker: *A Man on the Moon* by Andrew Chaikin. Her hands make brief, doubtful movements while she tells him how her job takes her to conferences all over the country, the whole world, in fact, because even in the rainforest they still get cancer. She says that it's hard to be apart from her family and Bill knows she is only pretending to read the charts that confirm his urine output is low today.

'My husband is funny,' she says. 'He calls me up at whatever hotel I'm in and tells me to open the window and look at the moon.'

'Oh?'

'He looks too, from the window at home. Doesn't matter where in the world you are, it's still the same moon.'

'Yes it is.'

'It connects us, see?'

'What? You both–? Oh. Okay. You look at the moon.'

The consultant oncologist blinks fast. She is offering him the moon as palliative care where chemo and radiotherapy have failed, but this is something a woman of medicine cannot say aloud; this is something Bill must come to understand for himself. Bill thinks *what the hell*? but the gesture is nice. Still, it is not reassuring to know that away from his hospital bed she is a person who misses her family and cries because some of her patients will die and her medical training cannot help them, although books might. A man, he thinks, would have kept this hidden. It is because of this that Bill feels compelled to pat the consultant oncologist's hand when she sets the book on his locker, but in doing so he makes things impossible. When it comes to the miracle of denial, whatever happens from this point on, he has overtaken her.

Bill is actually not much given to reading but he believes in good manners and here is the thing: once he lets go of the old scepticism a funny restlessness starts to waken in him with each new page. He inhales the raft of smells that must come from the fingerprints that have touched this book, hundreds of them, perfumed, nicotine stained, antiseptic, all impressed on the paper. It's good, maybe even a little addictive. He could put the book down but he could also read just one more paragraph. This new compulsion is prompted not by morphine but a wild ecstasy for the unknown and it is genuine, oh how it's genuine! Bill hasn't had a true feeling like this since he can't remember when. He isn't sure he understands it all correctly but still; faithfully he reads about the Gemini reconnaissance missions and how the moon's gravitational field meant the *Eagle* landed four miles from its aim point. The lunar surface is like a dirty beach, he learns, but also perfect as plaster of Paris, lonely and forbidding, or brilliant, the astronauts can't seem to decide. In many ways the consultant oncologist is a genius, but she is also wrong about one important thing: it is not the same moon wherever you are in the world. It is not even the same Earth.

There are nights when Bill falls asleep thinking he is inside Apollo 8, but being caught in the trajectory of the moon this way is no bad thing. It's a peaceful place to be. The motions of steering the rocket are as natural to him as eating and breathing. He closes his eyes and scans the radar for fatal mountain peaks, the ones that NASA hasn't charted, and all the while they push on through a splendid, silent world, every movement as easy as being underwater. Below are the Sea of Crises and the Marsh of Sleep, names he could never have imagined really existing. Deep space is lavender-coloured, spangled with exactly the sort of bright lights you'd see in a child's drawing and all Bill can think is how beautiful it really is, how ready he is for the impact.

His sister visits sometimes. They joke about the irony of his bed being in E Bay, but it can't dissipate the waiting or his worry that she isn't taking care of herself properly. Ellen Hare has a tendency towards depression. It started when she was sixteen and before clocking any of the standard teenage milestones Bill had gotten to be an expert in recognizing the signs, a certain swooping grace to the way Ellen walked, a preoccupation with facts and lists, as if through the magic of numbers she could hold back tides, storms, war. It isn't possible to rescue her from his hospital bed: when she comes to visit the change has occurred or it hasn't. Bill's own bad days are simple in comparison and centred mainly around intensive pain relief, but he cannot relieve Ellen of her pain and sometimes he is angry with her because she just seems to want to hold on to it all, and the intensity with which she does this is only possible because she doesn't know real pain, just like he hadn't known real pain, and if she did he can only think she'd want to get the fuck out of the pit she's been wallowing in for thirty nine years. The truth of it is that his love for Ellen is no more than the relief that comes when he is done with being angry, but love is a terrible thing like that, Bill thinks, love of any kind is no better than some scavenger that comes laughing out of the dark to feast on the kill.

On her next visit he says he's worried she's bit off-colour. Ellen Hare sweeps her hands, cupping the air in helpless parentheses by way of objection.

'I'm eating a lot of food out of packets,' she says. 'That rice you do in the microwave? Maybe that's it.'

'Well you look like shit, love. When I get out of here there's going to be some changes. You can't live on microwave rice.'

'It's surprisingly good,' she says and reaches for his hand from across the bed, holding it for a moment longer than is really required, because they both knew that although it is not yet impossible, it is increasingly unlikely that he will get out of here. A cellular blanket stretches out over the bed like the dim waters of the estuary he can see from his window at home and Ellen is distant, a dot in his eye, over on the other side just as she is in reality, in the house that was their grandparents' on the better side of the river. Royalty visits Ellen's side, as do film stars and the children of very rich people. But the estuary itself is just the visible statement of separation. Ellen has always been on the other side, although who is to say which side is the other and which the constant is anyone's guess. 'Make sure you get your five a day,' he tells her.' Just do this one thing for me.'

It doesn't really bother Bill that Ellen inherited the money. He chose another way, bikes, drink, the city and worse, and there was a time when he loved that life with a dirty, guiltless passion he wouldn't have given up for anybody. You could say that seeing how things have turned out, the version of the world where Ellen got the house, the bonds, a modest amount of shares in safe bets, is entirely correct. It's just that he has spent such a long time watching out for her you'd think he might be owed a little something. Over the years her fear has multiplied out of control like some invading virus, feeding first off her and then him and now the two of them have become fused into a new and ugly shape that wouldn't have been discovered had Ellen been the sort of girl who just married a guy from school and got a job in a call centre. Maybe a child would have given her some perspective.

The first few counselling sessions he went to after he was diagnosed were all about perspective. Mainly about how to achieve it and how to maintain it; maintaining it was traditionally the difficult part. The counsellor told him that it was normal to ask the question: why me? But this was not something Bill had ever asked. Why not him? This was a good response, a healthy attitude, he must have got it from some higher place, some kind of zen intuition. But he had not. He offered up the simple equation: you are the sort of boy who can't quite find his niche, you do some drugs, it equals you meet the wrong people, you do the wrong things. Then you meet one right person and everything changes. You change. You try to atone for your old, unenlightened ways. You become a Mentor to Young People, then an advisor to the police where your job is to point out the windows that can be jimmied open; you are particularly good at noticing the vulnerable cat flaps and letterboxes. You do other, subtler things like always making a point of giving way to drivers when it is your right to go, and even though the one right person didn't stick around long enough to notice your efforts and absolutely nothing is changed by any of this, the sum of it all is that at least you can say you tried. Actually it is quite a complex equation. Still. What did you try? Bill wants to ask his sister. Seriously, what did you try?

'There are cherry tomatoes in my hanging baskets,' he tells Ellen when she gets up to leave. 'Go and help yourself when you get home. Make sure you do.'

On Bill's side of the ward the doctors do their rounds twice daily to issue medications and advice, and not much changes until you are sent across the corridor for theatre. The light is low and claustrophobic there and the nurses hurry through a space punctuated by the slide of ventilators and infusion pumps, inhuman sounds. Bill knows this because sometimes he stops and listens when he makes his way to the shared toilets, imagining that he is moving through the holes left behind by these noises. It is a bit like swimming through the wreckage of a shipping disaster. The relief at finding yourself still there, able to swim, is tempered by the presence of things floating past, someone's shoes they will never wear outside again, or books so waterlogged that the words bear no resemblance to the language you've known all your life. These things tell of another kind of sadness, something the entire ocean can't dilute away. Bill moves through the debris and wonders how many things are falling down to the sea bed while he shuffles off for a crap.

There is a nurse, one of the younger ones, whom he likes. Newly qualified, he supposes, because she can only do observations and basic IV work. She has a name that you don't hear very often these days, but the morphine makes him forgetful and most of the time he can't think what, other than it is a flower name, not one of the prettier ones. She is a pretty girl though, with pre-Raphaelite hair and skin that seems hard and bright, like she is made of diamond. He is not so far gone that he hasn't realised this is merely a mirage of the drugs. Her cheeks are covered in a fine hair that makes him wonder about anorexia, but that could just be the drugs too, interfering with the ability of his retina to evenly process light and shade, as they also interfere with his ability to control his bladder and remember what day of the week it is. Although it has never been Bill's thing he can see why some men like their girls to wear nurses' uniforms, something about the knee length skirt and the little hats having the power to make the wearer both a person you would like to fuck and a person you wouldn't mind cleaning shit off your backside, and he guesses too that some men are imagining a place far away in a chintzy bedroom where girls are dressing up together and kissing it better.

The pretty nurse comes to his bedside with a tray, the usual syringes; clexane, diazepam, and a few empty phials for bloods. Cocktail hour, he murmurs and she bends over him, but only to pick up his arm and conduct the necessary formalities.

'William Hare,' she reads, holding his wrist and checking the name against the pad on the drugs trolley. 'Hospital number F3467008.'

'That's me,' he says. 'Most people call me Bill, love, but for you I'll make an exception. F34 is fine.'

'Well F34,' she says. 'I'm just going to give you your sedative. Would you assume the foetal position and lift your top buttock, please?'

The intimacy of these relationships startles him. These are girls who have seen inside you from every angle and there is no preparation, no forty minutes in front of the mirror to get ready for this kind of show. Nobody warns you about this when you are twenty-five. One day there will be strangers looking at your body, putting cameras inside you to rummage through the orchid pink gullies of your lower intestines, and when your veins collapse and someone comes running to flush them out, you will feel the same humiliation as losing a hard-on. Not that Bill would have liked to have been told. There was a time, before his legs became too weak to make the journey down to the hospital concourse, when he sank two pints of Pepsi in ten minutes and his gastrostomy bag exploded across two tables. The need to make his own mistakes, and by this he meant the grand rebellion of choosing his own diet, had been voracious, and he couldn't think why he had wanted to drink so much and so quickly. The unfortunate nurse who found herself first on the scene hooked him back up without a fuss but for Bill, horrified by an image of a girl in the neighbouring seat groping in his stomach juices and coke for her purse, that has never been the end of it. He can picture the purse now, some sort of geometric print and glistening, washed across the floor in the tide.

'Humour a dying man, can't you?' he says to the nurse, bracing himself against the cold sting of the hypodermic. 'Tell me a story. Any story.'

'What do you mean, like something made up?' The pretty nurse doesn't take her eye off the syringe, tongue just visible against her lip, concentrating on the glass like she's tapping for a seam of gold. Not everyone is as diligent as she. There are always rumours about how when the wards get too full the nurses start doling out air bubbles, straight to the heart and starting with the old folks first, but Bill doesn't believe them, watches her tapping away and thinks this must be how angels appear, not in an eruption of light but in a little blue uniform with breasts and everything.

'Yes. Isn't that what you call a story?'

'All right! I know what a story is. I just didn't get what you wanted it for.'

'To pass the time. To remind me of the other world.'

'The other world?'

'That's right.'

'I can't, anyway. I've only got five minutes.'

But something in his eye must break her and because the matron is busy and she reckons on actually having at least eight, nine minutes before anyone will really notice what she is doing, the nurse relents and sits on the side of his bed. 'Okay,' she says, shrugging. Her cheek is unexpectedly broken by an entire dimple that seems as impossible as a complete rainbow and suddenly, incredibly, she is involved. Bill has involved her in the business of his dying. For a minute he feels bad about this. He is no longer F3467008, and this will not help her much, even if it makes things a little better for him.

'Okay?' he says.

'I said it was okay! Now shoot. What kind of story do you want?'

'I'll go first to warm you up,' he says and he tells her about the Pepsi and the gastrostomy bag.

'That was Leila from ICU,' she says. 'Just about everyone's heard that one. So you're the Bagbuster. Lucky me.'

Bill assumes that Leila from ICU is not the girl with the purse, but this isn't made clear and he doesn't ask. He isn't sure in which version he'd have come off worst. The purse looked expensive and he supposes he should have offered to pay but now he feels a little buzz, having achieved infamy in this way. He tells the pretty nurse to go ahead, it's her turn, and she puts her head on one side, ducking it to the left shoulder and then the right while she thinks. It isn't hard to see this is the method by which she has won over men all her life, how she has made her father pay her phone bill or allow her to stay out late.

'Okay,' she says, finally. 'This isn't made up. But it is a good story. Are you ready?'

She tells him that a girl was killed in one of the nurses' houses. It was her boyfriend who did it, she says.

'It's always the boyfriend,' Bill says.

'So they say.'

One of the Sisters turns an interested circle through the bay and the pretty young nurse draws the curtains with such expertise that Bill knows that at some point in her life she has lived opposite a boy and that he was probably about two years older than her and attractive. The nurse's voice lowers.

'Her name was Mariella. They found her naked on the living room floor. I heard she'd been stabbed fifty times. I mean, that's anger.'

'I knew someone who got stabbed once,' Bill says, but the pretty nurse gives him a look that sucks the words he is about the say right back into a place where language doesn't exist and the only vessels for communication are hands, eyes, invisible gestures that are picked up like radar. The look suggests she suspects him of inventing a stabbed friend just to poach back centre stage. She tells him how the police came and talked to everyone in the murdered girl's block. 'I heard it from an agency girl,' she says. 'No word of a lie, there was this one detective and he actually said, "There's been a murder," you know like on TV. *There's been a murder*. I can't do the accent.'

Bill nods to show that he knows exactly what she means, even though she's right, she can't do the accent. 'Anyway, they arrested him,' she tells him. 'The boyfriend.'

Now Bill feels his body tense in one long contraction of longing to hear where this is going, because amazingly their positions have reversed and he is the one involved in her life, he is in the nurses' housing, he is stumbling into the room where there is a bloodied body on the floor; it is his voice on the phone to the police, *There's been a murder*. The longing builds into a wave. If he lets it go, it will smash him. He has seen how a wave can smash the human form right below his own house, down on the beach where it is dangerous to swim outside the flags. It is dangerous but people do it all the time and make it necessary for other people to risk their lives for them, all the time. He sees the wave coming. The wave is silent. It is vital he doesn't let it break. He is back in Apollo 8, leaving the wave behind.

'And then what?'

'That's it. That's the story.'

'That's it? That's what you call a story?'

'Well excuse me,' she says. 'I'm a nurse, not a fucking writer. Oh God. Are you going to report me for that?'

'No,' Bill says. 'I stirred it up a bit.'

There is a moment where he expects the nurse to leave and he is thinking of some way to say thank you for this thing she has just done for him, for being a light on a dark corridor in a way that is only barely a metaphor, when she says, 'Actually, it might not be the whole story.'

'Really?'

'There was something else I heard. I heard it wasn't the boyfriend at all, but some crazy patient. He reckoned he was in love with her or something, wouldn't leave her alone. It was okay while he was stuck in here but then he got better. She reported it and all, but the police said *they* couldn't do anything until *he* did something.'

'Is that true?'

The pretty nurse shrugs. 'It's what I heard.'

Something occurs to him as the nurse stands to go, parting

the curtains as if they are water, and for a minute he thinks he may have only imagined her and the body on the living room floor. But then she is in front of him again, waiting for him to speak. 'I'm not some crazy patient, you know,' he says finally, in case she is beginning to worry.

'I know,' she says, looping the cables of the emergency call button across the foot of his bed so he can reach it without leaning out. 'I know. I mean, I'm pretty sure I could take you out if I had to. No offence.'

Bill is nearly asleep when the same nurse comes back to check his sats, the sedative coursing through his system like a canoe flying over rapids. The feeling is like being drunk but stronger, wilder, as if it isn't just the room that's spinning but the whole world, and then he feels ridiculous because that's exactly what is happening, it's just that up until now it's been hard to believe. She tells him she's putting him on the oxygen for a while and with the first sharp new breath he suddenly feels many things in one, the billow of the pump, the cold, mineral smell of her skin as she cups the mask across his nose, the swing of the Earth. He sees the dent in her lip where health and safety regulations have demanded she remove a piercing. He sees that her eyes are not the same colour and that sometime in her youth she has had chickenpox and could not resist the urge to scratch.

It is hard to tell because he isn't even sure if this is sleep or a heightened state of wakefulness, but the pretty nurse is asking something. He only knows it is a question because her voice rises at the end of the sentence, but it doesn't seem to stop, as though she has stepped off the sentence onto a ladder that has no end, climbing up and up and further and further away until all that exists of her is her voice, her question. *Was that what you meant by the other world*? she is saying, or it might be *Are you comfortable*? It occurs to Bill that her story has only made him realise that there are things happening all the time in places he doesn't know by methods that would just never occur to a man like him, so perhaps it was exactly what he meant and also not what he meant at all. It is hard to be sure when he doesn't know what he has been asked. 'Yes, yes, perfect,' he says.

A short woman he doesn't recognise slams through the privacy curtain, followed by three students. 'We've got you on our emergency list for tomorrow,' she says brightly, as if offering him front row seats for the first game of the season. 'Someone will be along later to talk through the risks with you.'

The last student in the line steps forward to ask if Bill's next of kin are available.

'Risks?' Bill says but he is barely audible and the woman doesn't linger, sensing how all this grand despair seems to put off the students. They follow her across the central corridor and away in gauzy slow-motion to the other side of the ward. But the last student in the line turns back to Bill's bed, patting his pockets as if he has lost something, a pen, or his desire to be in this shadowed place. Bill shuts his eyes and breathes into the prism of the oxygen mask, out, out, out. Suddenly all his thoughts become questions. His only need is to be heard. If his voice is heard, he is living, he will continue to live.

'At the precise moment of death, will I be able to look

down at my body and see you trying to save me?'

'No.'

'No?'

'No, we don't think so.'

'But how can you know for sure?'

'We don't. But we're fairly sure.'

'Fairly?'

'About 99.9% sure. Personally…'

But the last student in the line doesn't say what he personally feels and Bill's relief at identifying his voice is like being lost at sea and seeing land, because as long as the words remained dispossessed he was afraid the cancer had reached his brain, or it was God speaking.

'How can that be?' Bill hears himself asking. 'We put a man on the moon but we don't know what happens when we die? What kind of half-assed scientists are you?'

'Science doesn't have all the answers,' the last student says as Bill opens his eyes. 'But it's better that way, don't you think, Mr Hare? Shit, my biro! Did you see it? They're like gold dust round here.'

In one of his deliriums Bill worries about the floor in his conservatory, which for some years has taken on an unpleasant smell in wet weather, he thinks possibly from when the dog was a puppy and still had accidents at night. The floor had been concrete at the time, the puppy having torn up the linoleum almost as soon as he arrived, so the urine soaked the floor in bright, phosphorescent circles that faded to shadows in seconds. He pictures the dog, surprised by the orbs of its own piss as if in a strange corruption of another old fable about the moon, where its reflection causes a fool to believe it has fallen into the lake. Bill imagines the fool striding into the cold, black water with a rope and harness, he feels the sudden freeze under his own skin and it's a strange, feinting sort of plunge as he finally goes under, looking for the moon. When he wakes up, two nurses are bending over him, changing the sheets. 'Don't leave it until the last minute next time,' the Nigerian one says sharply. 'Press your buzzer. Or better still, keep the urinal where you can reach it.'

He looks out of the window and lets his eye follow the dark shapes that move towards and away from the glass like the coloured beads of a kaleidoscope. He watches the tree branches lunge down to the grass below and then rear, leonine, up into the night breeze, while the nurses roll and wipe and fold down an angry set of hospital corners. One of the shapes breaks free, and it seems that on the approach to the window some sharpness to the Autumn air is planing it down and down and down until it has angles, shadows and only in the last minute does the shape become a bird.

'My dog,' he says, in a hot fright. 'Who is looking after my dog?' Then Ellen's voice and a blurred tang of ten-year-old Glenfiddich as she leans across, missing his hand when she says, 'The dog's dead, Billy-boy. He died, what, five years ago. We took his ashes up to Daymer Bay, don't you remember?'

'Can I tell you something?' Bill asks the pretty nurse in the morning, surprised and glad that she is still on duty to prep and move him across the ward for surgery. He would like to ask if there is any point to this latest procedure. More than that he would like to know whether or not he will even want the few extra months that carving out a section of his beleaguered liver might give him—but these are not medical questions, and Bill has been here long enough to understand that even consultants who use the moon as therapy will be unable, or unwilling to go into it. There is something else anyway, something subtler but more important that needs to be resolved, because the bottom line is that when he is on the table in two hours' time there will be no magic, only science, which hasn't got all the answers.

The impulse to tell is as urgent as anything he has ever known. He recalls that so many people die on the toilet because the need to defecate and an impending heart attack feel very much the same, and a worry fires up in him that either one of these two things might be about to happen. But minutes pass and neither does, so it is just the need to get the words out after all. The nurse sits on the edge of the bed and looks at him expectantly. After all that he doesn't know how to start. 'If I don't tell you then it's like...' he tries, but Bill cannot verbalise his fear on the first go.

'I know what you're saying,' she says. 'It's like if a butterfly flaps its wings.'

'It is?'

'No, it's not! It's something else. It's like if a tree falls in a forest. If a tree falls and nobody hears it, did it make a sound?'

You break my heart, he wants to say, because it is clear that human existence comes down to no more than this, a seesaw from the sublime to the ridiculous where everything is either absurd or happening in such deep isolation that no-one notices the moment of collapse. But he does not say it. Instead he motions for the urinal, heeding last night's warning.

'Wait,' she says. 'Maybe it *is* the butterfly.'

Bill Hare knows he can only be a disappointment now. He says that he worries he's built this up into something big and she gives him a little thumbs up, psyching him along. When he starts to talk he won't look at her, partly through embarrassment but also because, away over her shoulder he can actually see the past again, or at least a version of it where things seem to have become separated into their component parts for ease of classification. Under Nervous Apprehension he sees a parking meter, a bottle of wine. A weeping willow stands for Romance. He doesn't remember the kids with a bucket bong being under the willow but memory works in strange ways like that, holding back some of the details until you are ready to embrace them all. '*Romeo and Juliet*,' he begins, but it isn't much of a beginning. He finds there is less to say than he expected. Clare College Gardens. 1975. One of those outdoor theatre things. The nurse raises an eyebrow and he says, 'It wasn't my idea. You do these things for people, don't you?'

He says 'people' in the same way he says 'you do these things' but the pretty nurse sees it is not the same at all. She pats his hand. 'I'm listening,' she says. 'Take it away, mister.'

She is right about how hard it is to tell a story. He tries one opening and then another. When he settles on a final version, not the most detailed but accurate enough, the words come out of him in a rush like a flock of tiny demented birds. *It was dark and we were waiting for a lift I kept talking about the show I should have shut up but the night was like a miracle I wanted to tell someone the night was a miracle but those were the words I couldn't seem to find.* The words fly high and fast and free.

'This was a person you were in love with?'

'Loved,' is all he can say, relieved.

'But you didn't say anything.'

'No.'

'Couldn't you have…?'

'Moments go, baby,' he says.

Bill cannot tell her how things went from there like little movements down a mountain, from this pinnacle of breathless, violent joy to some half way limbo and then suddenly it was as if the two of them were home free and there were no more obstacles, except that a crucial, exploratory urge had left them. But perhaps the pretty nurse feels the hurt under his skin in the same, simple way plants pull water out of the earth, perhaps she senses that what he is saying is that this is his one experience of romantic love and after that night, he was all done. That was the damndest part, being done with love so soon and with such permanence.

'The lift turned up,' he says, instead. 'That's what happened.'

'So is that what you wanted to tell me?'

'Yeah, that's it.'

He is quiet for a minute, thinking of Stephen Hopkins in Clare College Gardens. Up until this morning he has only imagined them in the dark, under the trees in the same square foot of decanted light, but now he remembers that before this, at dusk, they were walking along the main road into the city and a dog ran out, a terrier or something equally small and snappy, scared the bejesus out of them. He remembers too that on Stephen Hopkins' thumb was a wart the size of a small button and all the while the dog was snapping in circles around them it seemed that if Bill pressed the button a connection might be made, a circuit completed. But when the shock died down and the dog ran off into the bushes there was no reason for their hands to be touching in any way. He had not pushed the button. More and more things, he realises, are going to become like this, memories without focus like inexpert photographs with no-one to identify them, just a guessing game of disparate months, weeks, days.

'I'm telling you this because you can't take it with you,' he says, suddenly afraid the pretty nurse doesn't understand. This is all he has to pass on and suddenly it seems so small. He has heard the words as if the first time—*this was someone you were in love with*—and he starts to laugh, but it is the same sort of laugh that he couldn't stop from coming when the doctor explained to him why it was too late for chemotherapy, a laugh pulled up from a sublimely lonely place. The doctor, who he feels he has come to know better than some of the people he unwillingly calls friends, had tapped across a map of his digestive organs with the eye of an expert jeweller finding imperfections on a set of stones you thought were going to be your fortune. *See this shadow on your liver? Our best guess is a haematoma but the whole thing is covered in cysts in any case; the function is critically impaired. Then there's your pancreas—shot to shit if I'm frank. Kidneys are good for another few months though*, and Bill had rolled on to his side on the leather sofa, laughing at his valiant renal system, laughing his way into a darkness that some of the worst people he has met wouldn't know. He laughs that way now.

'It's like a gift,' Bill says to the pretty nurse, sobering down. 'Maybe some of the other goners give you something proper, watches maybe. Does that ever happen?'

She doesn't answer, just holds his hand. 'You're not a goner,' she says softly.

'There was an owl hooting,' he says. 'It hooted just at the bit where Romeo goes into the tomb. He says something about the lightning before death. That was my friend's favourite line. If you're ever imagining that night, don't forget to put in the owl.'

The fluorescent strips spatter a yellow light that's enough to depress a person into giving up the ghost, which is pretty much how Bill imagined it would be on this side of the ward. The feeling of moving underwater has returned, but this time he is definitely swimming, stroking out into the cosmos alone where he can't feel the palsied motions of Apollo 8 anymore. He lets the anaesthetist do what he has to, stares up at the fading strips. There is some mild concern about his clotting levels but his kidneys are still good, which really is funny. Bill has never seen the point in the expression *funny ha ha or funny peculiar*. Even before he was diagnosed it seemed to him that most things are pretty peculiar, that so much consequence should be attributed to a life system that is only the result of random catastrophe after all.

Your sister is in the relatives' room, the pretty nurse mouths from the door and he shakes his head fast, God no, feeling a sudden panic that Ellen will come in and this odd little illusion he has created for himself will be ruined. 'See you on the other side then,' she says, turning to follow the anaesthetist, but Bill isn't done, won't let her go. He doesn't want to see what is on the other side. 'Sit with me,' he says. He wants her to know what it felt like to be standing out on the road at dusk, right there next to Stephen Hopkins, and in one crazed moment he wants her to find Stephen Hopkins and bring him here to this hospital, the middle-aged man that will be Stephen Hopkins sitting here with the old man that is William Hare, F347008. Instead, by some mean, alchemical process it comes out as: 'A girl your age doesn't know about love.'

The nurse won't accept this to be true. 'I happen to be in love this very minute,' she says.

'What are you, twenty? Twenty two?'

'Nineteen,' she rounds up.

'Then you don't know about love.'

'That's such a cliché,' she says, and her face tightens so quickly into an approximation of womanhood that he suspects she has to do this just to buy a lottery ticket.

'Okay, tell me,' Bill says gently and he really does want to know if it is possible to love and be loved from such a hallowed place as your teenage years. It seems a long time since he was nineteen, he can only suppose times have greatly changed. But he is glad to have asked, seeing how her face shimmers with the thrill of the tale. 'The most significant development in the history of love has been the Internet,' she tells him. This is how she met PJ, who has been so good for her confidence, always telling her she's beautiful, letting her meet all his friends. 'He takes pictures of me,' she tells him proudly, then blushes. 'His friends take pictures of me. I never thought I was anything special, but they say I could be a real model. It must be the light or something. You have to know how to use the light, right?' She is giddy with a sudden thought. 'I feel like Cheryl Cole, sometimes. PJ knows the right people, and I can't keep doing double shifts just to pay the rent, so maybe...' and the pretty nurse with diamond skin stares past Bill into a dream of money and paparazzi fanning her door.

'This boy,' Bill says slowly. 'How old is he?'

'PJ? He's not a boy. He's forty seven. And before you say it, it isn't... some kind of syndrome. I know what you're thinking. You know, like when you fall in love with your kidnapper. It's not like that.'

'Stockhausen's?' he says, taken aback, unsure if that is even the word he is looking for. That wasn't what I was thinking.

'Yeah, well, it isn't Stockhausen's.'

'It's love, right?'

'Yeah, that's exactly what it is. Love.'

Now the surgeons are late. The midday wind rolls in and Ellen Hare, crossing the hospital car park to the waiting taxi, is reminded that winter is coming. Inside the light is low, the pumps suck and slide. The radio plays *I don't want to talk about it* by Rod Stewart and Bill wonders how it is that all the songs you ever hear are about how hard it is to stop loving someone and never how impossible it can be to start. How you want to try but the fire won't light, or maybe sometimes there is no way of really knowing yourself and your own desires and that is why Stephen Hopkins never realised what it was they had between them.

'I'm glad I told you about PJ,' the pretty nurse is saying.'

I'd kind of been keeping it a secret, but what was it you said? You can't take it with you.'

'I did tell you that, didn't I?'

'For an old guy you're okay.'

'Yeah.'

'That bag thing could have happened to anyone. To tell you the truth the surgeons never put the tubes in far enough.'

He says, 'But why a secret?'

'Oh,' she says. 'Because people are so judgemental. It's just jealousy, I know that, but it feels so ugly.'

Groggily, Bill blinks at her. He flips what she is saying over in his mind, and over again and the thing she is saying feels heavy and smooth at the same time, like a ball-bearing he can't quite get a grip on.

'I felt out of my depth at first,' she says. 'I'm not saying I didn't. But you don't go anywhere if you're standing still, that's what PJ says.'

He's been lying there a while when suddenly Bill sees it coming, the dark side of the moon, and it's coming so fast he can sense the air backing up, the fear of the astronauts as the lunar orbit pulls Apollo 8 into the shadow and there it is, one enormous mountain that the best minds in astrophysics hadn't predicted. The Earth retreats at speed, so beautiful and so small. His mind won't stop. 'What are you saying?' he asks, squinting for her name badge. 'Ivy. Wait.' Ivy. What are you saying? Did someone hurt you? Ivy. He waits for the impact. The mountain keeps coming.

But Ivy is called to attend to a faecal impaction and Bill Hare has been transferred to theatre by the time she returns to the ward.

The path of least resistance

She was already talking to him when I came back from the store. I was getting lunch—for me, not Jim. Jim is the sort of person who can wait for a more appropriate time, the way a rat snake goes a whole week on a single egg, but I have to eat, what can I say? The bell rang when I pushed the door open, and I had the sudden knowledge of what it feels like to be a stranger. And then I realised this isn't particularly unusual, it's just that I'm the one who doesn't recognise me when I walk into a room.

They were admiring the Bergère armchair, the one with the damaged cane work that we were going to fix once, but now we just wanted people to want to fix themselves. Jim would explain to people how you could see past the damage if you just closed your eyes, imagined the way it would be piled with green velvet cushions fat with horsehair, as if closing your eyes was enough. He told people they were buying *the experience* and who's to say they didn't need that more. He had the girl closing her eyes, imagining. 'Fit for a King's mistress,' he was saying. She was saying, 'For a King's ransom?' and laughing.

With her eyes shut you could see she was young, much younger than me. At least seven, maybe eight years, which when only one of the people in comparison is thirty-something makes all the difference in the world. It's the difference between surprise and disappointment. I marvelled at the spaces around her eyes where the crow's feet weren't. You could tell that she didn't have anything pressing down on her from inside, nothing that showed on her face when she thought no-one was looking, the way a child thinks it's invisible when it closes its eyes. You could say it was vacant, her look, but in the way an empty apartment waits for the next occupant, a look into which things had not yet entered, not one where everything good inside had just deserted. And you could tell something else too, which was that even though it all looked spontaneous, this girl already knew what was going to happen next, so when she grabbed Jim's hand to steady herself it wasn't blindness but the last part of a move rehearsed in her head from the second her eyes closed, from when he began explaining to her about the fine balance between restoration and revamping. 'And which one's bad?' she was saying. 'Well, you don't want to lose the original character,' he was telling her, still holding her hand. 'You want to take the path of least resistance.'

Bea was her name. I would have forgotten but she made an actual point of helping me remember. Like the buzzing thing, she said in a carefully arranged but apparently casual way that told me she said this to everyone the first time. *Only with an A*. And then she and Jim laughed, but it was the continuation of a laugh that had begun a long time before I arrived and how do you join in with it, how do you find the point of intersection, it's like looking for the source of the Amazon, it's like walking into a show that has already started and you are thinking, is this Act II? is this the finale? All I can say is that you remember the strangest of things at the strangest of times. I was looking at Bea's hair brushing Jim's shoulder while they leant over the chair, laughing, and out of nowhere I remembered that;

$$\text{Force} = \frac{\text{Pressure}}{\text{Area}}$$

which is why the small things are the fatal ones; it's why a penny that falls from a skyscraper is like a bullet, or why a look can kill you when a bus can't. *So what are you*? I said. *A stiletto heel*? But there was no way of telling if I was talking to her or me, or if they were even words. It was like the way you'd talk to God and equally as hopeless. I felt the air break around me in a curve as though someone was shattering a bridge from her body to mine. I almost staggered backwards but Jim would have asked me, why are you walking like that? and then I would have had to explain physics to him and I wouldn't know where to start. Instead I told him I was going home to check on the dog.

He said, 'Do you need *me* to check on the dog?'

I told him no, that was why I had said I was going home to check on the dog.

There was a silence that I hadn't expected. It was the sort of silence you only experience when you are twelve years old and have done something unspeakable. You wait. How do you know which way things will go? 'Fuck,' he said. 'I knew this was going to happen.'

I turned to Bea, because officially she was a stranger and I thought she was probably expecting some kind of explanation. I said, 'Sadie needs medication.' And then, 'She's a Labrador,' which didn't explain anything at all. I was whispering, and Bea's eyes were still closed. She looked rapturous, as if every part of her being was pretending not to be there, so I was talking to nobody, I was invisible, I was mute.

'Would you give me the keys?' Jim said.

'But I'm happy to do it!'

'This is what you do, Lou,' he said. 'This is what you always do.'

'Christ, I'll check on the bloody dog!' Bea said, opening her eyes. Her face didn't look empty any more. It looked as if something had rushed in and arranged the space to look exactly the way it should have all along and when that happened I knew everything was going to change, or had maybe already changed, I was too tired to even care. And what made me most angry was that the thing I felt when I saw it was gratitude.

We all looked at the Bergère armchair. I put my hand on the broken cane work. *Leave it*, I wanted to say. *Leave it like this.* I waited for the next words. I wanted to know which way it would go. And the way it went was, she said: 'I'll give you fifty bucks. Would one of you help me carry this to the car?'

I curled my fingers into the caning, like I was dropping anchor. I closed my eyes. But it didn't work, I knew I was still there, we all of us knew I was still there.

We got the armchair last year, from the Recycling Centre. The day Jim found it was the day after Bobby's first anniversary. Or his birthday. Is there a specific word for the day you are born and die?

The chair was hidden behind some old industrial shelving and a broken BMX. I let Jim lead me to it, down asphalt pathways lined with the bits of other people's lives they didn't want, let him bring me to a stop using just the power of his breath. Here. He blindfolded me with his palms and I tried to look through them, through the glowing cells of his body and the sun and the corrugated iron boarding of the Recycling Centre to a place where the chair functioned the way it was supposed to function. That was the best I could do. What was I supposed to see? Something beautiful? Something made whole again? When he took his hands away I wanted to cry for all the broken things that ended up in the places where nobody wanted them. He presented it like a gift. I wanted to ask: 'Why are you giving me this when I asked for...

I asked for...

He said, 'This one's gold dust. If I fix this one up properly, I'll get at least twenty two hundred.' And I nodded, because who wouldn't want that?

And what if it isn't?

THE DEATH AND LIFE OF ROMANCE

You fall in love with a voice, with a book, a beard, or lack of. You, who feel nothing, who is a wasteland in a woman's body. You can't let any of this show on your face, even when he gets into your dreams and sets them on fire, but yes, one day you make a left turn instead of a right, you buy lunch at one café instead of another and you fall like a cliché, a stone into water. You have so much in common! You are academics. You teach classes that connect people with their inner poet. You have a mutual affinity for the second person and patisserie. Let's *split* the cake, you say, which roughly translates as: you have my heart forever. He won't, of course—no-one has anyone's heart that long. But from this point on you move around the city like an echo. It seems bizarre that natural selection has not stopped humanity loving this way, fatally, inconveniently, but this is how it goes.

You are a romantic who has officially renounced romance but keeps looking for it in hopeless places, the way you'd always have half an eye out for a cat that went missing years ago. It has always stood to reason that one day it was going to saunter in, bristle at your leg, lap milk like it owned the place. This much is probability. Still, you have a home to go to, and an apartment to clean, papers to grade. That much is fact.

THE THINGS THAT TIGERS WANT

On the terrace of a bar near the Zoologischer Garten you discuss literary beards. Right now, he's on a Chekhov. Hemingway is out of the question because of the way his neck resists all hair-growth. A pity.

The sounds of the animals in their make-believe worlds of jungles and ice floes, veldt and fynbos float high over the trees. The night moans of the tigers feel centuries old. He tells you he's leaving tomorrow. You quote Ondaatje because it's the only thing you can do.

'Damn it,' he says.

'Damn it,' you repeat.

You damn whatever you can get your mouths around. The sour and far-off stench of the wolf enclosure, the fucking cold. Time and the way it moves. Bright pink, rum-soaked cakes with ridiculous names. Students who do not read. Students who think they can sweet-talk you into changing their grades. That you missed a performance of Offenbach at the Zitadelle Spandau by ten days. You miss him and he is right there in front of you.

You tell him about the thing that made you angrier than anything else in the world, the thing you have never quite told anyone else. In the distance tigers bellow and you realise that even when you feel most crazy there is just no danger in anything you ever do.

'Let me see those fists,' he says and you bunch them up. You feel something small and tough, a fierce spirit forming inside you. A fighting spirit. Your breath freezes and flies hard into the night like blue fire djinn.

Somewhere in the dark you sense the tiger turning and pacing, prowling the length of its enclosure. More terrible than the growl is its sudden absence. The tiger's muscles, built for maximum efficiency in the thick, wet Sumatran heat, shiver and contract against a Mitteleuropean chill. You feel her wasted strength, her nostalgia for sharp jungle grass, the myth of home that, born in captivity, she knows only in her bones, the way eels follow currents blind until they emerge in the Sargasso.

The tiger's roar breaks free like a running man. It is a sound that is looking for something. The demands of the human heart are no different, you think. Even a tiger feels it. Even a tiger wants more than it already has.

ONE OF YOU IS MARRIED

The winter city at dusk, the hour of sinning lovers. But you are not lovers. There is no name for what you are. Your togetherness indulges no dangerous, expletive verbs, although you use them casually in conversation, sometimes, if not in reference to yourselves. You walk through evening shadows to the U-Bahn, moving from pool of light to lavender pool of light, and there is always a perfect four-inch gap between your hands, your shoulders; your heavy coats do not brush together and so the powder-snow remains untouched on woollen fibres, trembling with your footsteps like jasmine over water.

On one street, synthpop. Bach along another. You pass peeled-paint doors and posters for old operas. Your mind snapshots the shadows of dogs, a diamond necklace behind glass, the warm, grassy scent of horseshit on cobblestone. You catalogue it all with caution; you know what these kind of symbols can do. Yours is a profession that examines the fictional lives of fictional people; their hearts might not actually bleed or melt or commit any of the other atrocities that real ones claim to, but you know the odds aren't good. You've written essays on the subject of manifest yearning. When you teach *A Farewell to Arms* you have a kind of wild look about you, choreographing all that unquantifiable tragedy into a dance performed with your hands.

When he talks about Maupassant you note, appreciatively, that he too is fluent in the language of wild-gesture, his crazy-dramatic movements rivalling your own. If the universe is providing signs, here is a sign. His hands move the air around like he is operating an engine. It is imperative that an ocean of space rises and falls between you, always, but something in these wild-gestures...

You should have a contest of wild-gestures! A Gesture-Off. It would be sexier than it sounds. Something faintly threatening, like the Godfather Waltz, would play, faster and faster as you raised your arms, eyes flashing. He has that whole Byronic thing going on. It's hotter than Mercury.

When he asks, '*What is this*?' what you don't say is,

propinquity. You wave your hands in the dangerous way that means neither yes nor no, knowledge nor ignorance. He is only in the city for two weeks. Your Jewish friend would tell you, sometimes the harsh fact of life is that it is what it is. Urban Dictionary has another way to define this.

At the Hackescher Markt, you hesitate. He is the one to press the button that opens the doors, which might signify something, or it might not. This is your stop, where you are supposed to leave the train, after all.

IF YOU HAD READ LESS HEMINGWAY THIS PROBABLY WOULDN'T HAVE HAPPENED

'You're a Modernist,' he says, which explains everything. Only excessive consumption of Hemingway can be behind this violent hunger, the way it's not enough just to love—you have to also be broken into little pieces and reassembled with your ears attached to your cheeks or a rose where your mouth used to be. He teases you with fake French. You don't know how to tell him there are days when all you want is for a person to come along with a daiquiri, some passive-aggressive minimalist prose and a huge fish they just trapped with a net of their own design. This is hard to admit because women burned their bras to ensure this kind of thing doesn't happen. Maybe that makes you a terrible feminist, maybe it doesn't.

In your defence, at no point in this fantasy do you actually cook that fish. You don't arrange it on a plate, spoon feed anyone, kiss their feet or suck their cock while they slump in a chair and you slow-dance for their unilateral pleasure.

You just want someone to desire you in sentences of terse, heartbreaking simplicity. You suspect this need to tell and un-tell at the same time is, in fact, more than a little Postmodern, but seriously, he would whoop your ass if you opened that can of worms. Instead: you go with him to the airport. The howl of ascending Boeings reminds you how much you love to fly, that visceral keening of the plane as it prepares to take off translating inside you as both don't-leave-the-ground and make-me-soar. Manifest yearning, you think. Who of us can live with it? Something large and expanding pushed deep into a small space like a heart.

By way of goodbye he says, 'When I need a Modernist, I'll call you. In fake French.'

By way of goodbye you say, '*Ne me quitte pas*.' Your fake French is so good he doesn't comprehend. He heads for the departure gates, for his real life. At security he gives you the internationally recognised gesture indicating love, unrequited—which is to say, he doesn't turn around and fix you with a stare that pierces your heart but walks straight on, stopping only for the little see-through cosmetic bag the airlines make you use because if the twenty-first century has shown us anything, it's that it's possible, always possible that the whole world could at any moment come crashing down because of the simple things we hide in plain sight.

THE ESSENCE OF LONELINESS, OF *IN-DER-WELT-SEIN*

Your apartment in Rosenthaler Straße breathes the dark, competing smells of people who don't belong together. Across the street is a café fronted with bright red geraniums and metal tables. At night the tables disappear and people come to dance milonga where just ten years ago, Soviet military patrols enforced curfews and teenagers kissed in ugly, bullet-pocked stairwells.

He calls to tell you about a book he just read. In English. What this means is: he doesn't need you yet. You curl the telephone wire around your body like it is soft muslin. You swap anecdotes about work. You talk about seed cake like you are licking at each other's bodies, then you say goodbye with the awkwardness of strangers who have been forced to share an elevator for a floor too long.

What is this?

You head for the bathroom. You turn on the faucet, find your secret, expensive shampoo. Through orange-scented steam you trace the routes his fingers have never taken along your skin and your body becomes an aria, rising.

When your husband comes home, late, you pretend to be asleep. He smells of yeast and rain—not verdant valley rain but the kind that hits concrete and absorbs all the unwanted smells of the city. You lie very still. The cure for everything—vertigo, a fox outside your burrow—is to lie still, that much our instinct knows. The stillness is a way of repelling all the movement of the world, the moving dust, the moving curtains, even the moving fibres of the rug that bend like grass under his feet. Your husband shoulder-barges the bookshelves and curses, like he does most nights, but still: you do not move until he makes you.

THE LETTER YOU WILL NEVER SEND

You think about how wild you could be if you chose and realise instead that what you have become instead is completely motionless. Even the silver-winter sky is moving faster than you. You are outside your body, appraising it, giving it directions like an untrained animal. Like a playwright, heartbroken by the actors' interpretation of his words, you want to cry for the distance between the thing you intended to be and the thing it turns out that you are.

You want to say to your husband, don't do it like that. You're not unblocking a drain. You move your hand in the direction of where he is frantically looking for change, playing a bit of Spanish guitar, what even is it? You move your legs differently, up a bit, back a bit. You imagine gestures of extraordinary wildness that bring another mouth to yours, summon them deep in your prefrontal cortex. Cortex isn't erotic. You lose it. Your husband sighs, a slow sigh of desire exhausted, so one of you is satisfied. One of you is as good as it gets.

You get up from the bed, sit at your desk and write. You fuck the hell out of your fake-French speaking friend with words you will never send. You try soft words, love-words, sharp syllables that hurt like pebbles under feet, the broken, meandering mountain-path of the first person present continuous. You pour out these feelings like thick cream, filling a jug that flows over and over the tulipwood desk. You take the sheets of paper, fold the words away like gristle into a napkin. Then you stand at the window, open it, cup the folded paper into your palm and set it free. It falls straight to the November slush on the sidewalk. Figures.

The shadows inside the milonga cafe turn fast and the room swells with a sad song of violins and longing. Soon the city will be full of the light it celebrates by leading golden-haired girls down streets paved with gingerbread. Just a little bit Wicker Man, you think. You imagine catching snowflakes on your tongue, or burning inside a giant effigy. You wonder how it is possible that human existence can be so weird, so beautiful, arbitrary, animal, perfect and terrible, so pointless and yet something you would hang on to at all costs, through all suffering, for as long as it takes.

THE THEORY OF THE UNIVERSE *IN SILICO*, FULL OF SENTIENT BEINGS THAT DO NOT KNOW THEY ARE IN A SIMULATION

Even a tiger's heart, you feel, rebels against this.

WAS THERE EVER A TIME WHEN A HUMAN BEING DIDN'T WANT SOMETHING MORE THAN IT ALREADY HAD?

It's rushing down fast from the Baltic—winter. You hear its feet. You remember when, years ago, you caught the morning train to Stralsund, from there the ferry to Rügen Island; you stood on deck watching the hull spray diamonds through a drum-tight sea. For non-specific reasons that was a day when you thought anything might be possible. It's not even nostalgia, what you're feeling. It's a suspicion that the spotty kid simulating your life in his futuristic garage has got bored, downed a cup of some kind of life-enhancing energy serum and left you on auto while he masturbates to the latest thing in space porn.

The night sky above your apartment prickles with light. You make a wish on the brightest star you can find. Only as you're closing the windows to shut out the damn milonga do you see the star is in fact a landing aircraft. You don't retract the wish because—who knows.

The next time he calls, he asks about the tigers in the Zoologischer Garten. You tell him how the tiger enclosure is currently closed because a keeper was mauled to death. That's a real conversation killer. You are both silent, imagining, maybe, the light of the tiger's green eyes. The wreckage of desire. The kind of death that comes from doing something that meant the world to you, once.

'Damn it,' he says.

'Damn it,' you say back.

Everything you cannot say with any of the spoken languages of the known world you translate into wild-gesture. It doesn't matter that he can't see you. This is the way humanity says everything it has no words for.

What is this?

It is what it is.

And what if it isn't?

To the men I have tried to seduce with prose–

–I make no apology.

But it's hard to give up bad habits, like drinking before the bar opens, or checking your horoscope. If there's a Mars-Jupiter trine combined with a Spring Equinox, it helps to know it's really going to screw everything. Shoot me. There are worse vices.

And what is fiction if not the healing lie?

I don't recommend Hemingway, Proust or *Anna Karenina*, for reasons that if you've received such passages, you'll no doubt be aware. Those lines from *The Shipping News*, the ones where diamonds crack in hot goat's blood, how many times have I typed them to myself? I know I've a tendency towards a prose of repression, but—I'm whispering here—aren't we always in the wrong story? The one that mustn't fit, isn't that the one where we feel most alive?

You will summon true love with Ondaatje, a fortune cookie predicted, years before.

If I have tried to seduce you with prose, come close and listen. Come. The truth is I was showing you how to seduce *me*. The question everyone asks about the location of the clitoris is the wrong question. What I am saying is: tell me about winds. Fuck me in the violets above Fiesole.

And if I had used poetry–?

Once I flew across the Indian Ocean, hard and fast into the light from the oncoming dawn. I thought of you—so dangerous—and what I told myself was: *how much safer my life* if I just gave nothing away.

This is Eden

Naturally, Adam gets the drinks in. Once it fell to me to fight change into the cigarette machine, but times have changed; even here you can no longer smoke inside. You can't stick a postage stamp on an envelope with the queen's head upside down or touch the trilithons at Stonehenge, although there is an old by-law that still permits a pregnant woman to piss in a policeman's helmet if the need takes her.

The music is fast and loud, just right for slamming Tequila, but it is a myth that you will find a worm at the end of the bottle; only for a gimmick is it sold *con gusano*. Adam smiles at the waitress and says, 'Dickens walks into a bar and orders a Martini. The bartender asks: Olive or Twist?'

The waitress sucks the piercing in her lip as she serves him. She smoothes down the bar towel and works her fingers through the blur of her dark hair, and I am reminded of lights flashing in muddy water. *Min min* lights, the light of the dead. She plucks at the jasmine that rests above her ear. 'I don't get it,' she says.

Maybe he explains it to her while I am checking in my

bag. When I come back he is lining up shots, squeezing the lime, rationing salt, and all the time the waitress smiles lazily, her mouth wide and pretty, the easy way he likes. It's taken ten minutes and they're on first name terms. I stand just out of view and watch them as if it is not the rest room that I have been to but the other side of the world, as if there is something I have forgotten in some room far away, something important, and I cannot for the life of me remember what it is I am missing.

For all the things you can say about him, Adam is surprisingly unoriginal. And so it is to alcohol and women that the guilty man turns.

This is how it begins. A man walks into a bar.

(Ouch. You'd think he would have seen it.)

The Flaming Sword Motel is lapped on four sides by water, dark, stone-filled water, clotted and dirty with a hundred years of secrets. But when the clouds cover the moon only the crying of the gulls says you are no longer on land. It goes without saying that the rules are different here. Across the world are places like this, set adrift like rogue asteroids, the ones humanity is so terrified of.

The Sword attracts what it likes to think of as a select crowd; writers, painters, magicians, illusionists and, rumour has it, a princess or two, all of whom will wait hours for the causeway to telescope out through the waves before crossing to the island to dance their asses off until morning. An ex-Pope took control of the pool table for eleven days straight, back in the day when the winner still stayed on. The gossips say that Houdini was a regular, but the only trace of him now is the unpaid tab behind the bar. Even the air is heavy under the weight of words. When you want another drink you have to push past playwrights who orbit the bar like stars, greedy for each other's light. A good night is one where you make it to the bar without being stabbed in the eye with a quill.

We sit high on stools and suck lemons that dry our mouths and make us wink suggestively at strangers. There is a breeze this evening and a party at the bar for Penelope's divorce. Penelope dances on the table, a chain of flowers round her neck, the plastic kind you would wear at a luau. She has a glass in each hand, a man nibbling the toes of each stilettoed foot. People know her here as something of a homebird. But tonight there she is in heels, shining and free, grinding it to a shimmering bass.

Beyond the window the causeway glints like slate and the surf breaks from a cold horizon. Tiny fish hurtle out into the dark. It is the age of the sea, not its depth that scares me. You can smell it in the room when you pick up an ashtray, and you can feel it move the hairs of your arm, like the nervous memory of an amputated limb.

There is a story going round that a local man went down to the shore one night where there were rumours of a mermaid in the vicinity. At first he thought it was an oystercatcher, spiralling downwards to the seabed like a blade. Then he saw the white-green flash of her skin, the cold gleam of the fish's human eye. He waited until the moon was full and fucked her in the dunes, the sand like a hot razor against the delicate flicking of her scales. But it is well enough understood, the strength of the lovesickness that a man feels for the things he cannot have. He knew he already had her body, the pulse of her cold-blooded limbs forced close to him as a rumour, the possession of her guaranteed. But rather than let her body return to the sea, he chopped off her tail and with it took her soul, or so the story goes. He stood there on the beach, they say, surprised by his own triumph, her heart held tight in his palm like the coin in a magic trick while the waves turned red with blood.

It is a new moon tonight.

Some people say this a good time to mend things, unless it falls on a Saturday when it portends twenty days of wind. Others say that if you turn over the coins in your pocket you'll have luck in all your affairs. I knew a man who would, no matter where he went in the world, send home a photograph of the night sky, scrawled on the back the words; look at the moon!

There is a place I sometimes dream about, a place at the head of two rivers facing to the east; an ancient place of dark rain and grey moonlight. It's a place that reminds me of the coming of a storm, the feeling that everything has an edge, that everything ends somewhere.

'It's not what you think,' Adam is saying, downing his third shot. The fourth he spills across the bar, a steady, sticky ooze that snakes out over the square of mango wood that separates us from the optics behind. 'It wasn't *love*.'

Of the ten steps to rekindling romance, we have reached an impasse at number three: creating a relationship vision. Step Four is learning to know your lover. Step Five is learning to know yourself. The former, I suspect, will not be a problem because I have always found it easier to understand the absurdity of another person than I do my own.

'Of course it wasn't love,' I tell him. Only in films do people find themselves fucking someone who isn't their wife out of *love*. For the rest of us it's boredom, the need to feel the burn of a stranger's hotel room carpet against the crest of our spine a symptom of there being little else to do. The shape of the heart has long been painted on the signs above brothels, but it is not a symbol of love. It is the shape of a woman, swollen and heavy with the intolerable weight of desire, the breasts and the open cunt calling out like a song and a warning, to rich men who wanted the smell of dirty sweat and foreign perfume at their fingers, to sailors, who tattooed it on their arms and colonised the world with the lie that the heart is an organ of romance. Here is what the man on the beach did not understand. The mermaid. She gave away nothing when she left her heart behind.

From the end of the bar a man in black Levis and evening gloves signals to us, sizing us up. It's an interesting combination that makes me want to ask him about his childhood, but something in the way he spears a cocktail stick through an olive, holding it in front his face like a tiny lantern, makes me think better of it. 'You together?' he says. For a minute the olive spins around the stick, smooth and purple, like some kind of nascent planet. Then it's gone, the oil dribbling down his goatee.

'We're together,' I say, because once it was true. The man's eyelids are painted bottle green. He is wearing lipstick. He is older than either of us, much older, but the music he asks the barman for is something with a beat only the young can keep up with.

'Eve,' I say, and he kisses my outstretched hand. The weight of my fingers feels alien in the soft, kid prism of his gloved palm.

'What are you drinking, Eve?' he says.

The Mai Tais arrive with a little lake around the tray, delivered with a flourish. I drink mine the way Don the Beachcomber intended: with aniseed and a garnish of soft, fleshy fruits. Adam is a traditionalist and asks for his over shaved ice with a sprig of mint. Strictly speaking, accepting drinks from strangers is exactly the kind of thing we have agreed not to do while following the programme; all forms of compulsive behaviour, including gambling, lying, Facebook and Ebay, are to be avoided. But it is only advice and I have ignored better.

'Don't tell me,' I say, turning to Adam, because we still have unfinished business. I am suddenly exhausted. 'Don't tell me. She wasn't better, just different.'

The man in the black gloves looks interested. 'Don't answer that one,' he warns Adam, smudging hashish resin along the line of an unrolled cigarette. But Adam is already face down in his glass, a mint leaf hanging from his mouth, and the man lights up, tips his head back, the smoke ascending like a plume and the smell puts me in a kind of dream where I can see my son, both my sons, and my first dog, all of us looking out towards the ocean, where the air is purple and violent as a storm comes in from across the mountains. But in just one lightning flash I am at school, sitting my midterm History paper. The invigilator stares and when I look down I am naked.

'You want some?'

I open my eyes and the man is holding out the joint, delicately, like I have seen people hold fragile animals and scale models of famous battle heroes. There is a faint scent of soap about him, lavender cut with something hard and antiseptic. Close up to the bowl I can see the olives are marinated in little pieces of garlic. The way he holds it, the joint, it is almost tender.

'I ever tell you what I love about you?' Adam says, but he passes out before he can tell me what it is he loves. And the man in the black gloves is persistent. 'So what did he do?' he asks. 'Forget your birthday?' He sighs a hot bubble of air across the bar.

'We're trying marriage guidance,' I say and laugh, because suddenly I have heard it aloud.

'Waste of fucking time,' he says, flexing his hand around a dirty coin. 'But it's up to you. What the hell.' He rolls the penny across his knuckles. 'Heads you make it work,' he says. 'Tails you move on and give someone else a shot.'

'I don't make decisions based on chance.'

'All decisions are based on chance.'

He puts his head on one side, challenges me to consider the possibility that this is the only true option. 'Good girl,' he says, beckoning the barman over. 'I'm buying. Anything you like.'

In this watery place we have to learn to separate the sound of the waves from the sound made by the things that undo us. Always it is words—my weakness. I am only half aware that the man in black gloves is speaking to me, his mouth pressed to the skin under my ear. Outside, he is saying. Come outside, baby.

The roar of the night surf pounds like blood in my ears as the man in the black gloves fucks me hard against the stone wall, the way you would stoke a fire, efficiently, and with purpose. For all his fury his mouth is soft, surprised by its own urgent, animal calls. There you are, he says, pushing his gloved fingers stiff against my tongue. There you are. *There you are*.

His skin on my skin like I am a ball of plutonium, rolled between his thumbs. I half expect to see burns, shiny and slick, searing my thighs, my cunt, everywhere he has been.

I think of another joke just as he comes. It might be that I even tell it aloud. Descartes. That's how it starts. Descartes walks into a bar and the bartender asks, 'Would you like a beer?' 'I think not!' Descartes says, and vanishes.

Afterwards he offers me the obligatory half-smoked cigarette and I inhale with gratitude, looking out to sea as if I am scanning for a landmark that will root me somewhere, just this once. But there is only water. There aren't even any stars. Here is the true meaning of un-coordinated. The column of smoke leaves my mouth like a bird ascending and I imagine that far away someone will see it and perhaps for them it will be a different kind of sign, a thrilling sign that connects them to something real that is happening far away, that will make them feel more real in return.

'I gave up,' I tell him apologetically, as he buckles and rebuckles his belt with a speed that tells me I'm not the first to have felt the sharp ridges of the sea wall at the Flaming Sword Motel grind into the small of my back.

'No you didn't,' he says, and takes the cigarette back, stubs it out, gently, lovingly against the stone.

❧

You don't need me to tell you that other worlds exist beyond this one.

I ended up in Eden for what you now call crimes against humanity, but the truth is that a man simply wouldn't have had the courage to do what I did. Visiting hours are three until eight and all appointments have to be made a fortnight in advance—subject to cancellation if it is not in the interests of the residents' emotional health. You come to see the patients through what we joke is the servants' entrance. A river flows through the main gates and if you follow its banks from outside in, it is said you will forget your soul and can never leave. You want to say it's bullshit. But then are those who'll tell you that the soul is constantly trying to escape and you just don't realise it; it is why they insist on saying 'bless you' after a sneeze.

My name means *life*, but you probably know me better as an afterthought, something brought into being by necessity and not desire, although if I am particularly unlucky you will think of me as the source of all human agony—and that's fine. There is nothing ceremonious about being crafted from a rib; you take whatever glory you can get. This morning a newscaster reported that female promiscuity is the cause of recent volcanic eruptions that have disrupted the globe and caused untold economic hardship. I should be offended, but I have always known I have the power to make the earth move.

There was light, and then the heavens and last came Earth, the sudden hush of the sea, and following that, animals, birds and man. I came last. I came at the world from the shadows, hooded and shackled. I arrived vowing to take as much as I could and give back as little as I could get away with.

In those early days some things got a little muddled; it was only to be expected, given the high maintenance design for a planet where a shift of one degree on its axis could spell mass extinction. There were times when the light seemed to be water and the water seemed a dangerous, black light and I was drawn to it, because that is the inherent property of both water and darkness: they pull everything in. Something I did not expect: when the teething troubles were ironed out and the elements became fixed, the darkness would linger, like a beautiful woman passing a mirror. Something I expected even less: that when it comes to the crunch we are more afraid to be ordinary than tragic.

Cassandra calls it Scarlett O'Hara syndrome, where you don't want something until you absolutely can't have it, and when you realise it you'll fight to the death to make sure no-one else can have it either. Cassie, dropped on her head as a baby, thinks she has a gift, the kind that has half the new girls queuing up for relationship advice and the wardens asking for lottery numbers. On long evenings when there are no visitors at all she entertains me not with stories of past exploits, but visions of the future. I try to tell her that all this soothsaying is old hat. Seeing is not knowledge, I tell her, the future isn't fixed. It's constantly being assembled, you could change everything at any moment. Or perhaps everything could change you. Love, even. Who said that—that love is a form of becoming?

There's none like the wise for making you feel a little crazy. But she nods at me, weighing up what I have to say. I am on a roll now. I am enjoying myself. What I know hollows me out, I say. It's an unbearable thing. It's like being given the date and time of your death. I would prefer blindness to that. Sure, says Cassie. Tell that to Tiresias. For a minute I am almost ashamed, thinking of that incident at the baths, the scandal that followed, the rights and wrongs of it all. But I am flippant to a fault. Peeping Terry? I say. Well he's another one who knows shit.

But the strange patterns of the moonlight hitting the trees make me stop for a moment, wonder if the things I know and the things Cassie sees aren't the same after all.

Evening, and the light fails across the garden as it always does at this time. I wade into the quiet water of the river and there is nothing but sky and the last glimpse of the sun, which has been dying since the very moment it came into being. I wear lotus in my hair and smile for the groundsman who appreciates my buoyancy in a way that I, from what once they called the Myspace angle, never could. I take a breath and sink under, roused, as I am every time, by the cold.

I have changed considerably over the years. There was a man who painted me once—in Vienna; we'll call him Gus.

He said he wanted to see me as a blonde and who was I to disagree with an artist, despite the inevitable jokes? Did you hear the one about the beautiful girl and the man who kept her chained to the kitchen sink? She ripped him limb from limb, then ate his balls with a nice Chianti.

He began me in pencil, a little rough, and then slowly, wildly, beneath his fingers I was formed, in layers of ruby and cobalt and linseed. Although it took me by surprise, I have to say the finished product caught something about me that others have missed. My smile hard, like a diamond. I knew I wasn't the only woman he loved. I suppose he was thinking of us all as he moved the brush across canvas, the blaze of one girl's skin, the sly eye of another. There is a song I heard once that he might have appreciated; the words no doubt will come to me.

He liked to work almost naked, Gus, in sandals and a toga, going commando as he strode about the studio like a Roman emperor. *Whoever wants to know something about me*, he said, *ought to look carefully at my pictures*. There are rumours that he painted his most famous works using a telescope, but all I will say is—that's not what he liked me to call it.

Curfew comes through hollows of jasmine. White buds peel down from the branches and tremble like the moon in running water. The sky is a canal of stars. Who said that lilacs were the smell of nightfall? Onyx is the colour of darkness. I know of women who will not wear an onyx ring for fear it will keep them awake at night.

There is a girl, resident here for a decade or more, who waits in the trees just to listen for the sound of her own voice.

It was taken away from her, so the rumour goes, because she used it to tell stories that distracted a wife from her husband's marital indiscretions. You can see her sometimes, shouting obscenities into the night in the hope that someone will hear and love her in the same fiery way the husband loved his mistress. More often than not the words return to her, hesitantly through the dark, like doves learning to fly home.

Another girl hides in the sky to watch over her baby son, both of them flung across the heavens in the shape of a bear because she was found fucking a god. In one session they asked us all what the moral of her story might be. There was a show of hands. The girl who was picked answered: 'Be careful you don't get caught.'

A little bit of Monica in my life, a little bit of Erica by my side. You know that song? Is that Lou Bega? I think so. It's Lou Bega, the song I was trying to remember.

The shining sky and the roof of the world. This is what I see when I float on my back in the river. Sometimes I stay there until out across the world the tides turn and what is washed into the pool is water a thousand years old. Water from the Taurus mountains, cool and smooth across my skin like raw silk. From Mesopotamia a hot and heavy wind. In my mouth the taste of snake's blood. The bile of memory. The sounds of the bees, which are the sounds of purpose. Something I ask myself: what of all the sounds in the universe we are yet to hear?

So this is Eden. We are allowed out on day release, under

supervision, once a month. The last place I chose to go was a beach not far from here, at the end of a winding road dripping with white alliums. The crime rate around this place is surprisingly high; here and there you see a gate kicked in, a car keyed from front to back. But then, through the pines you see it, the glare of the sun on the causeway and the water below, something clean, renewed. With each curve of the narrow lanes we turned into the sun, leaving behind houses, telegraph poles, refuse trucks; with each curve I turned my face away, thinking this would be the moment I was blinded.

Let me tell you something. Eden is no paradise. It's a Category C, a rehabilitation centre, a place where men try to hide us from the rest of the world while we contemplate what they think of as our misdemeanours. But other worlds exist beyond this one. Other crimes. Other tides.

The barman does a trick with a cocktail umbrella and a bottle of Schnapps, and I clap along with the rest, mainly because I find it impossible to observe disappointment. Momentarily awake, Adam raises a clumsy toast above his head, but the glass strikes his cheekbone and a waterfall of ice and Curaçao liqueur sprays across the table . '*Maita'i roa ae*!' says the barman, and Adam vomits a full moon onto the dark boards of the motel floor. A silk hibiscus flower floats on its tide. For a minute we stare at it; the barman and I. Then he calls out, '*Naga*! Get your ass here *now*!' and the dark-haired waitress comes out with a mop and an attitude.

The barman has a crush on Adam, that much is clear.

The name on his badge says Jon, but he isn't Jon. The real Jon has been absent without leave for some time, he tells us. Last anyone heard he was pining for some sixteen-year-old who won't fuck him. The barman says if there's anything Jon won't walk away from, it's a challenge.

He tosses the umbrella again and lets it sail down until it catches in the neck of the bottle. He does it without looking at the bottle, he does it looking at Adam with the smile of a person who has nothing to lose. For a moment I am genuinely entranced. The umbrella curves around in the tiny thermal. I watch it float on a current of bright air. Magic kept alive in the sureness of the barman's hand.

The waitress Naga mops the floor, moving through the crowd as if she is parting the Red Sea. She has the sort of beauty that worries men and makes women angry, the sort that women spend a long time looking at to be sure that what she possesses is only beauty and not something more troubling. What I look at is the camber of her hips, taking her away out the back with the mop and the hibiscus circling in her bucket. Hypnotic. Serpentine. She frowns, meeting my gaze. Then she is gone and the door slams, and opens, and slams, as though the molecules of everything around her are getting out of the way just to let her past. I go to the bathroom. I look in the mirror and fix my hair. I see that rouging my cheeks is academic now.

For a while we drink and dance, sometimes almost touching, sometimes alone, like islands in a dirty sea. Now and then I turn and Adam is there, behind me. 'I'm drunk,' he says. 'Eve, baby, I am so drunk.' He shuts his eyes. Tonight I am not drunk at all. I am perfectly lucid. When I'm sure Adam is looking I reach for the shoulders of the man in the black gloves, feeling the bones through the silk shirt that billows from his Levis like something is trying to get out from under his skin. There are moments when I want to lean in and press my head to the domed green moons of this stranger's eyelids. But as soon as I feel that I think: it's not up to me to *make* Adam jealous.

I sway for a moment and then the man in black is gone, sitting up at the bar as if he hadn't moved away. 'Who knows this game?' he is saying, clicking his fingers to the barman who is not called Jon. He lines up nine glasses and swings nine measures of vodka across the tops, glass to glass like dominoes. Then he adds a tenth and fills it from the tap. He nods at the waitress, Naga, who obligingly places the shots on a tray. To some she adds lemons, others a lime. Some are untouched. When she's finished, the glasses are in a circle, random. One of the glasses is water, she tells us. But which one?

'Eve,' he says. 'You'll play. Who else is in?'

The men want to play for forfeits, the women prefer to call them dares. Penelope's girls are up for it in the beginning. The first round, the waitress loses. Her eyes fix pointedly on the man in the black gloves, but he doesn't look at her, kaleidoscopes another round of glasses out across the tray instead, shrugging. She shoots him another glare. 'I don't do dares,' she says finally and returns to the mop, the steady removal of the day's traces from the floor. Penelope is out next and the men chant while she removes her bra without working her way out of the tiny dress into which she's squeezed herself. I stare at her breasts, low and luminous against the plastic shudder of the luau flowers, the darkness in their centre telling me that at some point or other she has been a mother. A long laugh roars through the divorce party and what I am reminded of is a school of sharks. A shiver of sharks is the true collective. How appropriate this is for animals that have to keep moving or die.

After a while, only Adam and the man in black are still playing the game, most of the glasses discarded, the girls quieter now, sitting in the loose, tired positions of those who are waiting for someone else's signal to allow them to leave. But Adam is restless too. 'You know what,' he says, standing up. 'Your game bores the crap out of me. Eve, go get your bag. We're out of here.'

'The tide's in,' says the man in the black gloves, flipping open his wallet. 'We're here until morning. Let's make it interesting.' He offers me another joint. 'You'll like this,' he says, bringing it to his nose, licking the tip. 'Manali. Produced by hand.'

Adam tosses a bill on the bar. 'Okay,' he says. 'Okay. Ten says I don't get the water.' But something in the older man's glittered eye seems to hold him. He throws in another ten. The room grows with the silence. Adam sucks in his breath and adds three more notes to the pile. 'Come on. Fifty. Fifty says I don't get the water.'

'Fifty it is,' says the man in black.

But when he drinks, for the first time, Adam gets the water.

'It had to happen,' I say. The man in black says nothing, slides the bills across the bar and pockets them. Adam is nonplussed. 'Fine,' he says. 'A hundred says I don't get the water twice.'

But when he drinks, it's water in the glass. In the air is the edge of something suspended, like a note held by a single instrument while the rest of the orchestra breathes. There was a concert I once saw like this, where between movements, a wave of clapping travelled through half the audience before someone realised the mistake. Then something occurs to me, something I think I have been aware of for some time, the thing I have been trying to remember. The Flaming Sword is not what it used to be, but there are still some high profile visitors. 'Is that who I think it is?' I say to the barman, shrugging my shoulder towards the man in black as he sets up another round. 'It's not–?' But the barman doesn't answer. He looks up, seems to notice me for the first time. 'Why? You interested?' he says.

'Double or quits,' the gloved man is saying to Adam. 'But it's my risk. What are the odds you'll get the water three times in a row?'

The odds don't change, I want to tell him, but Adam's already drinking, grimacing just a little. It's water, and the man in black smiles, counting his money.

'You want to go again?' he says.

'Stop it,' says the waitress. 'He's drunk. You're taking advantage.'

'Bullshit. You're fine, aren't you, sir?' the stranger asks Adam, expertly shuffling the next round of glasses about the tray. 'See, Naga? He's fine.'

I want to tell him not to be stupid. Adam. But it is almost

a relief, this curiosity, my own unchecked need to see how far he will go.

How far turns out to be six and a half thousand dollars, half on the table outright and the rest in chits made out of napkins. He doesn't—we don't—have this kind of money and Adam knows it. But he sits quietly, like a child waiting for instruction.

'Okay,' says the man in black, when he has finished counting the napkins. He tips the contents of all but two of the glasses into the ice bucket on the bar, stacks the empty glasses high. He beckons to the waitress. He looks Adam straight in the eye. 'It's been an expensive night,' he says, 'and I'm going to give you a chance to sleep easy. Those odds weren't on your side.' He looks a little distressed at the thought. The concern, it almost seems genuine. 'So I'm changing the rules. I want to reward those kind of odds. One last shot. Fifty-fifty. You get the water again, the money's yours. All yours. But here it is. I don't play for free. You can keep your money, but'—and now he looks squarely at me. 'I get your wife.'

'Fuck you do,' Adam says and laughs. But the man in black is not laughing. He looks a little confused. He scratches his neck, purses his lips into a knot.

'You get the water, you keep your money and I get your wife,' he repeats. He passes the glasses to the waitress who scowls into the tray. 'I'm being generous here.'

'Eve,' Adam says, helplessly. 'Eve?'

It was only money, I want to say. But I don't.

And it is only now that I am aware the bar of the Flaming Sword Motel is almost empty.

The barman who is not called Jon has started to cash up, scrolling the till receipt into a little leather purse. He is one of those people whose tongue basks on the bottom lip to indicate concentration. 'I don't want any trouble,' he says.

'No trouble,' says the man in black. But suddenly there are three men standing behind him and the air is not the same. The optics behind the bar glint like savage rubies under the security light. One of the men puts a hand on Adam's arm and as he jerks it away it seems, for the first time, that he too has noticed the way the man in black looks familiar and distant in the same glance, the way your own self seems to retreat and resurface in a photograph of yourself at an age you cannot physically remember. 'Say,' the man says brightly, as if he has just thought of the idea, 'What if your charming wife picks for you? Eve? Which of the glasses is it?'

Adam rubs his eyes, dazed. 'This is ridiculous,' he says. 'It's just a goddamn game.' But he looks at the wad of money in front of him and he sits down, because it turns out the decision is not so hard to make after all. 'You can't do this,' he says, without looking up.

'You bet your life I can,' says the man in black. 'Or your wife's. Just so we're clear. So which one is it to be? Eve?'

There are so many misconceptions in the world. For example: you think it was an apple, my downfall, but when did anyone ever *actually* tell you that?

I look at the two glasses in front of me and try to sense it, to feel the one that contains the water, as if that is going to make any kind of difference to anything. I close my eyes and think of the movements of her hand, the waitress, the shapes that she drew across the tray, again and again and again. The tap of silver against glass. And suddenly I am back outside the Flaming Sword, where bottles tumble from the wheelie bins, and the dogs snarl and scavenge on leftovers, and down across the causeway the tide is turning. What washes over the stones is water a thousand years old. From the east comes a current of ice. From the west, a hot and heavy wind. I think of the tail of that mermaid, thrashing in the dunes while her severed body convulses, cursed with the muscular memory of swimming. And there is the waitress, Naga, silhouetted against the sea wall, her cigarette a fevered dot against the heavy red line of her lips.

'You got something on you,' she says sullenly, stepping into the light. 'Looks like blood.' She gestures underneath my ear with a movement that looks for all the world as if she is miming slitting my throat. I see the shape of her hands, the silver ring that curls about her index finger, weighing it down, strangling it. There is a garnet for the snake's eye, the little forked tongue licking at her nail in a slice of aquamarine. I touch my hand to my neck. 'It's lipstick,' I say with relief, bringing my hand up to my face. 'It's just a bit of lipstick.'

She looks at me for a minute longer than is necessary, trying to read something in my face, something that disappoints her and evades translation. When she finally speaks, the words are familiar, not déjà vu but pulled up from somewhere old, and real, as if recorded and replayed from an ancient airwave. 'You got some nerve, girl,' she says. 'Messing with my man right in front of me.'

I open my eyes. Some things you cannot unknow. The fact that I will spend a lifetime, many lifetimes, yearning—it means I have little to lose. So I choose a glass, and I say, 'This one.' I hold the cold glass for a minute, circling it in my hand, tilting, rotating. I say it again, louder. 'Definitely this one.' Then I throw it in Adam's face and he sobers up very fast.

I turn around and walk to the door, to the pitch dark skyline, to the edge of the water. And as I walk it comes to me, from far away, the distant feeling of something ripe in my hand. How I threw it lightly into the air, like a ball and I how I caught it hard, like a stone. Well as well this apple as any other.

I remember—

And there goes the knowledge coursing through me like a disease, and there goes the juice running down my chin; in my mind I can taste it, bitter and old, and in my head there it is again, that feeling, young and sweet, and what I feel, what I taste, is the moment the fruit breaks in my mouth and I *know*. I walk to the door and I think of it, how I bit down hard.

I think of it now, and I bite and I bite and I bite.

What we talk about when we talk about rockets in the night

We're four storeys up in a fin-de-siècle café in the Old Town, eating cake and talking about bad sex scenes, because we're writers and we feel that gives us the...well, you know the rest. It's -10° Celsius outside and we're keeping warm thinking of those authors who get their literary kicks from bulbous salutations and barrel-rolling breasts, but here's what we're learning: not one of these heavyweights can hold a candle, or a stray rocket, to Peter's back catalogue.

Peter's not from here. Like Auden says, you need to move your mouth both ways at once to pronounce the name of his hometown. Even the weather in that place is romantic. Even the wind is poetry. But there's nothing poetic in the story he's telling us about some librarian he hooked up with a couple of years back, although it's rhythmic, I'll give him that, the tinny *pfft pfft pfft* of his spoon hitting the teacup, the occasional word semibreved for impact.

'She wants it in the ass,' he's saying. 'She wants it the way Brando does Maria Schneider in *Last Tango in Paris*. But we don't have butter. There's olive oil, she's shouting from the bedroom, but it's dark, and I'm naked in her kitchen and I know her kid's asleep right across the hall. So I just grab a bottle and run, and I'm slapping it over us, I'm seven layers deep in her before it hits me. Zeta. Those motherfuckers don't just make oil.' He pauses. 'They make vinegar too.'

'Seven layers deep?' Tomas interrupts. 'Seriously.'

'Who ordered this coffee?' I ask.

'Silvie Szczepaniak,' Peter says. 'She'll be here in a minute.'

'Silvie Szczepaniak?'

He checks his phone. 'Any minute now.'

I've never heard of this girl, and truthfully, I'm a little upset. This isn't how our lunches work. It's a special dynamic, the power of three, ancient and elemental. It's a kind of pact. But even before I've figured out how to object with some dignity a brunette in leggings and an outsized t-shirt walks in, and the way their faces change, I know it's her.

Silvie Szczepaniak is Polish and delightful. Her eyes are watery green like a Bengal tiger, but she has this crazy mess of dark hair that makes me think of the selkies my grandmother said stole men from the fishing villages up in the far North. The giant t-shirt just adds to the feeling of someone ready to leave behind their own skin.

'We're talking bad sex,' Peter says, by way of introduction. 'Not rockets in the night, the fucking worst experiences you've had. Coffee?' He nudges forward the glass, now starred with lacy beads of condensation.

Silvie Szczepaniak sits down. There's a dry, mineral smell about her like she's made of snow, *lössnö* they call it here, the kind that looks pretty but can all of a sudden be dangerous.

'Is it decaf?' she says. 'I only drink decaf.'

It isn't. I want to feel sorry for Silvie Szczepaniak, but it's hard. I can't imagine it possible she's ever known anything less than heaven. Still, it seems as though she's putting genuine effort into mustering up something to share, although how can I say for sure when for me what's coming to mind is the guy who told me to 'go easy on the testes' and I'm wondering if that even counts as a sexual experience. It was barely an experience. It really was the limit of what happened between us. I didn't so much as breathe on his cock. The closest I got was my hands passing above, making a couple of promising sweeps like a magician about to pull a scarf away to reveal a rabbit.

Silvie Szczepaniak twists her hair around her finger. Shakes her head as if she's trying to dislodge something inside. If she finds this whole situation weird she doesn't show it. 'The fucking worst or the worst fucking?' she asks. Her eyes close. 'Max Lindher. From… I forget where. He liked me to jam carrots up his arse while I… you know.'

'Another arse story?' Tomas says, but Silvie Szczepaniak gives him the look of a leopard seal advancing down on a fairy penguin and he shuts right up.

'Or he'd tell me to get my finger up there,' she continues, 'and look for this little bump. The prostate? It's there somewhere, he'd say. Higher. You've got to *reach*. And you know what?' Silvie Szczepaniak says, 'I couldn't ever find it. There was just nowhere left to reach. Is that the measure of a shitty relationship, when you're rummaging in a guy's arsehole and there isn't anywhere else to go?'

There's a moment where it seems like any one of us might

be about to laugh, but none of us does. It's as if at exactly the same second we've all realised there is nothing to be said out loud to that. Not in the faded elegance of this place. There are velvet curtains. There's a whole table of superior leaf tea. The kitchen staff clink the silverware and outside the snow just presses right on down to the street four storeys below. It's as if we've all fallen clean out of the known universe into a moonlit place where Silvie Szczepaniak's hands stretch up and up in forensic supplication and we're floating past like we're pages someone just ripped out of a book, and the real world is just a faraway picture, an old polaroid in a box, the *yrsnö* whipping my hair around like I'm some kind of luminous comet, and I'm bucking my hips like those women who dance *taranta* to drive out the poison of the wolf spider. I tear my blouse open. I'm shaking as if I have a fever. My breasts are hard as little onions and I'm rubbing them until they're blood-red, I'm crying, *Praise my face, damn it, praise it*! My mouth is overflowing marzipan and cream. And I realise I'm looking straight at Silvie Szczepaniak, backlit and gilded from the winter sun at the window, all that dark selkie beauty crammed inside her spilling out like a whole river from a tiny glass, the soft plum flesh of her cunt its starfish taste her thighs my God I want to say *pearlescent*, and that's the moment I stop falling. My chair hits the table and the coffee glass floods clots of hot foam onto my lap, and the sound I make is sharp and feral, like something wounded out in the woods.

No-one says anything. No-one moves even when the waitress comes to clean up the coffee. We are stilled by those human sounds all around us. It's as if we really have nowhere to go. I'm not even sure if we are thinking of Silvie Szczepaniak's elegant fingers inside this man Max Lindher or if we are imagining something new now. We've entered a different world and all I can think of is that it's my turn coming up and I have never known enough of anybody to have a story, even a bad one, to tell.

About the author

Lucy Durneen lectures in English and Creative Writing in Plymouth, England, and is Assistant Editor of the literary journal Short Fiction. Her short stories, poetry and non-fiction have appeared in *World Literature Today, The Manchester Review, The Letters Page, The Lightship Anthology* and *Litro*, amongst other places. She has been shortlisted four times for the Bridport Prize, Highly Commended in the 2014 Manchester Fiction Prize, and nominated for a Pushcart Prize.

Acknowledgements

I would like to thank Angela Smith, whose trust in, and patience with, my writing allowed this book to come into being. For their support, offered in various, unswerving ways, thank you to all my colleagues at Plymouth University, particularly Anthony Caleshu, Rachel Christofides, Gerard Donovan, whose advice is always bang on the money, and Miriam Darlington, for the lentils and the listening ear. Martin Goodman, Paul Lawley, Tony Lopez; thank you too.

One event shaped this collection more than any other—the 13th International Conference on the Short Story in English, held in Vienna in 2014. For their various roles in getting me there, and in doing so changing everything, enormous thanks to Mary Joannou, Maurice Lee, Susan Lohafer, Farah Mendlesohn, and Sylvia Petter, and to the inimitable Vienna Crew itself—especially Rebekah Clarkson, Lauren B. Davis, Nancy Freund Fraser, Rhoda Greaves, Sandra Jensen, Cate Kennedy, Paul McVeigh, Jeremy Osborne, and Cameron Raynes for their feedback, support, belief, and impeccable deployment of music/poetry when required. For explaining manifest yearning, thank you Robert Olen Butler. These stories yearn harder because of one workshop.

With deep love to my Alpha Sisters, Inês Lampreia, Maria McManus, and Mel Perry, and to the Coracle/ Kultivera team who provided an early audience for some of these pieces, and Scandinavian hygge in which to repair them; Colm Ó Ciarnáin, Magnus Grehn, Peter Nyberg, Ulrika Sätervik, and Dominic Williams, thank you. For cheering this project on, often child care, often cake, thank you Lisa Coyte and Hannah Lees. Inspiration and encouragement comes from so many places; thank you Eleanor Birkett, James Churchill, Stu Connor, Harry Dell, Philip Webb Gregg, Sarah Haider, Keeley Middleton, Leonardo Valladares Pacheco de Oliveira, Gürkan Özturan, Lindsey Parry, Mike Sloman, Uppahar Subba, Shaista Tayabali, Julia Trahair, Rose Waheed, Hugh Warwick, Sarah Whateley, Tory Young. Thank you for giving these *desiderio manifesto* an Italian voice, Greta Galimberti. For solving the riddle of the title, Tom Vowler. For giving me a piggery of one's own, and a laptop to steer by, David and Michéle Lambert. John Andrews and Jude Summers—it began with you. To all the editors who first published individual stories from the collection—thank you for taking a chance on them, and for your continued support; Dan Coxon, Tomek Dzido, Pippa Goldschmidt & Tania Hershman, Sam Jordison, Christopher James, and Jon McGregor, you are especially wonderful in this regard.

To the Muses: for your unparalleled appreciation of limerence—thank you, Friðrik Solnés Jónsson. And Adnan Mahmutović, beta-reader and story-prompter extraordinaire; *hvala* will have to cut it this time.

My soul sister Caterina. *Grazie mille. Tu mi ispiri.*

Thank you, Louise Ells, for telling me to *emerge*. Caron Freeborn, who kept me fed in soup and poems, and my long-suffering family, Alan and Angela Dawes, Kate and Anton Mezzone, Karen Dennison, Ted and Margaret Dennison; you all got me here in ways varied and vital. To my grandmother, thank you for telling me to set sail from the safe harbour; one reason this book exists.

The MidnightSun team, Peter Cassidy, Allan Taylor, Lynette Washington, Kim Lock and Zena Shapter you are quite amazing. And Anna Solding, master publisher, life coach, inspiration, without whom this simply would never have happened, for saying 'We can do whatever we want.' We can. We are.

To those who cannot hear my thanks; to Mary, to Chris. You are present in these words.

My boys. My girl. Thank you always.

And Vincent. He knows why.

Stories

'Time is a river without banks' was first published as a Galley Beggar Single in April 2016, and reprinted in *Two Thirds North* in May 2016.

'Noli me tangere' was shortlisted for the Bridport Prize 2014, the Storgy Short Story Prize in 2015 and first published in *Storgy*, (March 2015.)

'Everything beautiful is far away' was shortlisted for the Bridport Prize 2010 and the Cinnamon Press Short Story Prize 2011. An earlier draft of this story was first published in *In Terra Pax and Other Stories*, (Cinnamon Press, 2012)

'The smallest of things' (with the title 'The Way Things Are Done') was given an Honourable Mention in *Glimmer Train*'s Very Short Fiction Award, May 2014, shortlisted for the Bridport Prize 2014, and published by *The Jellyfish Review* in November 2016.

'The old madness and the sea' was first published in *Short Fiction*, September 2012

'Countdown' was first published online with *Tube-Flash* in October 2014

'Let it out' was shortlisted for the Lightship Short Story Prize 2011 and first published in *The Lightship Anthology* 1, (Alma Books, 2011.)

'In response to your call' was first published in *The Letters Page*, October 2014, with the title 'No-one to turn to and ask.'

'They dedicated the mass for the soul of Paolo Alonso' was a Top 25 Honourable Mention in *Glimmer Train*'s Open Fiction Award, September 2010.

'All the things' was first published in *Hotel Amerika* in August, 2016.

'It wasn't Stockhausen's' was a Top 25 Honourable Mention in *Glimmer Train*'s Open Fiction Award September 2009, longlisted for the *Short Fiction* Short Story Prize 2010 and first published in *The Manchester Review*, 2011.

'The path of least resistance' was a Top 25 Honourable Mention in *Glimmer Train*'s Very Short Fiction Award July 2013 and first published in *I Am Because You Are*, (Freight Books, 2015.)

'And what if it isn't' was Highly Commended in the Manchester Fiction Prize 2014 and first published in *Litro* as 'Wild Gestures', (December 2014), reprinted under the title, 'And what if it isn't' in *Two Thirds North*, April 2015, and translated into Italian for *La Tigre di Carta*, July 2016.

'To the men I have tried to seduce with prose–' was shortlisted for the Bath Flash Fiction Award, October 2015.

'What we talk about when we talk about rockets in the night' was first published in *The Jellyfish Review*, July 2016, and nominated for a Pushcart Prize.

MidnightSun

Lucy Durneen's collection of stories brings one deep into the terrain of the yearning heart. Hearts that have not loved, or hearts that love unevenly, fretfully. There are bodies that betray, health that oscillates; the decrescendo of existence. And characters who are 'too alive', or 'always in the wrong story', captured between the exquisite sharpness of reality and the dark dance of the mind.

Catherine McNamara, author of *Pelt and other stories*

This is an intriguing collection of short stories where things are seldom what they seem and characters are preoccupied by their past actions. Shaped less by plot than by precise and evocative imagery, they are psychologically acute portraits of people dealing with grief or change. With titles such as 'The Old Madness and the Sea' and 'Everything Beautiful is Far Away', the ocean is a recurrent image, the ebb and flow of its tides mirroring the undertow of suppressed emotions. The stories can be bleakly funny; when one character's heart freezes over, she compares the spread of ice with the spread of cancer, coolly remarking that both seem inevitable if you don't heed the standard warnings. They can be unexpectedly chilling, too. In 'Noli Me Tangere', a young girl's apparently spontaneous response to a local boy's invitation while holidaying in Italy turns out to have a much more self-serving and sinister purpose. There is something vicious at the heart of these stories, something dark which unfurls and unsettles. In UK writer Lucy Durneen, MidnightSun has found someone who revels in the imaginative possibilities of language while simultaneously exploring its inability to adequately express what people mean. Distinguished by its measured yet speculative style, these stories will appeal to readers of Cate Kennedy and Mary Gaitskill.

Books+Publishing